Four Buses

In the snow, Turkey–Iranian border, Philip Wadd

Four Buses

A collection of short stories and flash fiction

GAIL ALDWIN

arial

To: DCA, 1964

Published by arial
20a Glyde Path Road, Dorchester, Dorset DT1 1XE

First published 2012 by arial

ISBN: 978-0-9574172-0-5

British Library Cataloguing in Publication Data
A catalogue record for this book is available from the British Library

Front cover and frontispiece images by Philip Wadds

Set in 11.5 pt Garamond

Printed and bound in England by CPI Group (UK) Ltd, Croydon, CR0 4YY

Contents

Preface

Following a flash fiction workshop delivered by Tania Hershman and Vanessa Gebbie as part of the Open Book Festival in Bridport 2011, I began writing flash fiction as an antidote to the slog of completing a manuscript. Since then I've had some of my flash fiction published in print anthologies and other work has appeared on-line. On 16 May 2012, I joined Calum Kerr, the director of National Flash Fiction Day, and with other flash fiction writers we celebrated the launch event in Southampton. During the 32nd Winchester Writers' Conference it was announced by Geoff Fisher of CPI Anthony Rowe that I had won first place in the 'Slim Volume, Small Edition' competition. The prize for my entry, which comprised a variety of flash fiction stories, is the printing of the collection that you now hold.

Acknowledgements

In my journey to become a published writer, I've enjoyed considerable support from fellow writers and I'd like to thank Rachel, Louisa, Sarah, Daniel, Lucy, Jo, Fiona and Geraldine. The Wimborne Writers' Group and Cerne Abbas Readers have been generous with their advice and encouragement. I'd like to thank Julie Musk at Roving Press for her help in editing this collection. Feedback from the followers of my blog and #FridayFlash, the on-line writing community, has been invaluable.

About the Author

Gail Aldwin was born in London and when she was twenty she travelled from London to Kathmandu on a converted double decker bus. During the next few years she worked overseas in a range of jobs including waitressing, teaching English and office work. When she returned to the United Kingdom, she studied to become a primary school teacher. In 2006, she moved with her husband and children to Dorset, where she now appreciates life in the county town. Gail writes novels, short stories and flash fiction around gritty themes such as racism, homelessness, depression and alcoholism. Through her work she aims to celebrate personal resilience. In *What the Dickens? magazine*, Gail has a regular column that answers writers' questions. For further information, please visit http://gailaldwin.wordpress.com.

Wait There

Daylight stings my eyes when my Mum opens the curtains but I'm glad the morning's here. I stretch star-shaped under the duvet. Mum's meddling with my things and the wardrobe door creaks. I hope she hasn't chosen a dress for me to wear.

'I've laid out some clothes for you,' she says. 'Your Dad's coming at nine o'clock.'

'I'll be up in a minute.'

'You better have some breakfast before you go. You know what your Dad's like., he'll probably forget you need to eat.'

'It only happened once.' That was the time we walked the Ridgeway without a map. Dad said a strong sense of direction ran in the family and he tapped his nose. I followed him through a field of bullocks, and we waded the stream. I was starving by the time I got home and Mum never forgave him.

Ignoring my Mum's choice, I take a pair of shorts from the drawer and put on a hoody. When I go into the kitchen, Mum raises her eyebrows towards the ceiling and tuts. The porridge is steaming in a bowl and I trickle honey over.

'That'll keep you going,' she says. 'You might want to think about putting on some jeans.'

'Okay.' I was going to change anyway but it's always fun to annoy my mother.

It's nearly ten o'clock when the pounding on the door begins. First he uses the knocker, then he bangs his fist on the frame. His shadow through the obscured glass is crumpled. Mum gives me a hug and kisses my hair then guides me forwards. There's no way she's letting him in the house, so I release the latch and step onto the porch. His eyes are glassy and have a liquorice centre. He slings his arm across my shoulder and squeezes me. There's a damp smell about him and his jumper's creased.

'I thought we'd catch the train down to the coast.' He pulls some gum from his pocket and offers me a bit. I shake my head. 'You remember when I built that massive sandcastle, the largest one on the beach?'

'Yeah, it was my island when the sea came in.'

'Yeah.' Dad kicks a stone along the pavement and we bump shoulders and hips as he lurches. At the station, no-one's on duty, so we dodge the barrier and chase along the steps as the train pulls in. We grab a couple of seats and I stare out of the window. Dad finds yesterday's newspaper in the bin and begins to read.

When we get there, I sit on the shingle and I look out to sea. The sky's a great wad of grey and the sea's shiny and silver. Dad's skimming stones or trying to – the best he can manage is three bounces. He yells and beckons me over, but I prefer sitting and watching. He runs up the beach and collapses in a breathless pile.

'You want a Coke?' he asks. 'I'm dying of thirst.'

'Okay.'

'I'll go and buy us a couple of drinks.'

'I'll come with you, keep you company.'

'There's no need, Susie. The shop's just over there.' He waves an arm towards the buildings lined up on the other side of the putting green, then he's on his feet and walking backwards. 'Wait there. You need to save my place.'

A man in an anorak throws a stick and his dog bounds along and back again as if he's on a piece of elastic. There's a family camped on a strip of sand. The tent's puffed and the windmills on the sandcastles whirl. Shuffling on the stones, I turn around, hoping to see Dad, but he's not about. He's been gone ages and I wonder if he's been run over or mugged. Maybe he's lying in a gutter somewhere, unable to move. The worry makes my shoulders tense and I cling onto my knees, holding myself together. My hair flaps around my shoulders but there's a bit of warmth when the sun peeps around the clouds. I wonder whether I should stay put or go looking for him. He told me to wait, so I suppose I must.

I'm stiff as a frozen fish when the gulls arrive. They give me a flash of their lizard eyes and I stamp my foot to scare them off. A mother pushes a buggy along the path and she stops when she sees me. She calls over, asking if I'm all right. Nodding, I wave my arm, then she shrugs and walks on. I tap the screen of my mobile, the phone's useless without any credit, but at least it tells the time. I guess he's been gone a couple of hours. Standing up, I shield my eyes and study the road. I search for a medium-height man, the sort that should be spending Sunday with his daughter.

Finally he comes, reeling towards me as I huddle on the stones. There's not a can of Coke in sight but a fag hangs between his lips, ash patterning his jumper.

'Sour face Susie.' He slumps on the stones then lies back and puts his hands behind his head. His face and neck are a rosy pink, the colour clashing with his red hair.

'Forget the Coke, did you?'

'Shit. I knew there was something.' Already his eyelids are drooping and his breath becomes noisy.

I stand up and walk around him, my shadow splitting his head from his body. Turning to check that no-one's watching, I aim my foot at his shin and give him a bloody good kick. He splutters awake.

'Love you, Susie.' As soon as my name leaves his lips, Dad's eyes are closing again.

'You too, Dad.' I give another kick, my toes jamming inside my trainers. This time he rolls over.

Putting my hands in my pockets, I walk along the road until I come to a telephone box. There's no surprise in my mum's voice when she takes the reverse charge call.

'Wait there, darling,' she says. 'I'm coming to get you.'

Hoping

Jet strides onto the treads then sprints down the escalator. With his arms extended, he turns like a champion and shouts for Liv to follow. She takes a step then glides towards him. At the bottom, Liv tumbles against his chest and Jet swings his arm around her while she tucks her hand into the back pocket of his jeans. They cling together and take each step in time, heading towards the benches. She catches glimpses of their reflection in the shop windows, admires the way he's gelled his hair, wishes her legs were thinner in those short-shorts.

They sit together, their thighs touching, and Liv whips out a mirror to check on her lip-gloss. While she's busy, Clara sidles up and Jet jiggles along the seat to make room, tapping the bench beside him. She takes her place like a foot servant to the king, and Jet shows Liv his back while he whispers in Clara's ear. Liv gets to her feet and wobbles on her heels then folds her arms and stares. Clara gets the message and slips away, pretending to look for a friend.

'I'll buy the drinks.' Liv points to the café and, squeezing her eyelids shut, she hopes to feel the weight of his arm across her shoulders.

Conversation

I throw off the covers and slide onto the cool side of the bed. The slick of varnish on my tea tells me Jem left for work ages ago. Twisting my fingers through the bars on the bedstead, I lever by body into a sitting position and adjust the pillows behind my back. My pregnant belly rises like the mound of a hill and beyond it the tops of my painted toenails show. In the corner, the Moses basket sits on its trestle frame, a trim of broderie anglaise ruffles the edge and baby-grows for a newborn are folded inside. On a peg hangs the length of Kente cloth, a gift for the baby. The blocks of weave in pea-green and gold dazzle.

Pulling back the silky nightdress, I study the pearly skin that stretches over the baby parcel. Blue veins stripe the surface and around the edges, flecks of stretch marks pattern. As I watch, the baby turns, moving a limb so that my stomach bulges. There's not much room inside there now, not like when she first started dancing. With my finger like a paintbrush, I draw a pattern on my leavened loaf and as my nail catches I quiver at the sensation. I plan a conversation with my baby in the womb and think about the things she'll need to know. Shall I teach my child the points of the compass so that she'll never get lost? Shall I scribe lines of poetry so she'll learn the puzzle of words? Shall I tap a drumbeat to give her rhythm? Instead I cup the babe between my spread fingers and hold her tight. She's the globe of the world between my hands.

I wonder what she'll look like, my baby-to-be. Will she have a ski-jump nose like the rest of my family, or will she have the squat, flat shape of Jem's? I doubt she'll have my fair hair that glints in the sunlight but a shock of black, all bouncy like a sheep's coat. There are blue eyes that run in my line but she'll have brown ones, where the whites are creamy and rich. She might have freckles, pretty dots across her cheeks, and she'll have a shade of skin between the two of us, like cinnamon powder stirred into a cappuccino's froth.

When I was growing up, my parents called our neighbours wogs yet I played with the children to annoy my dad, and I'd go round to their house for tea, to spite my mum. We children were friends together, except when we fell out, that's when I'd call them the darkies from along the street. But things have changed, haven't they? This is a community where there's tolerance and respect. My child won't be called half-caste as if she's half a person with half a life. And she won't be mixed race, like she's a mixed-up human being. She'll be herself: the best of me and the best of Jem.

White Socks

I tie the cord of my dressing gown. I've grown so much the sleeves come right up to my elbows. Mummy says it doesn't matter that it's a bit small, it's not as if the neighbours will see. Walking down a couple of stairs, I loop the fraying edge of the carpet around my toes. The fourth step's warm from the pipes underneath and I stand, listening for the gurgle from the boiler. There's a smell of burnt toast coming from the kitchen. Mummy says bugger and the sash window screeches – I bet she's scraping the bread and tipping the black crumbs outside.

There's no school this week so me and Paul are taking it easy. He's reading a comic in bed but Mummy has to get up because there's Daddy to look after. It's not long until he leaves for work. The coins in his jacket clink as he swings it off the back of his chair and he finds his coat hanging on the stand. He sees me on the stairs but he doesn't say anything – he just calls goodbye to Mummy. When he's gone, I know it's safe to go all the way down.

The door to the lounge is closed. This is unusual, we don't normally shut doors in our house. Grandma says we ought to be ashamed of ourselves for all the heat we waste, but when she's not around, Mummy says it doesn't matter and that they're more important things to worry about. I push the door and peak inside. The Christmas tree's in the corner, and when I switch the light on a few bits of foil twinkle. The floor's covered with carrier bags, and tissue paper, ribbon and felt. There's one green bag with gold writing from Marks and Spencer. Lined up by the wall are a couple of baskets. 'Paul' is written in red letters on one, the other says 'Sus', that must be for me, it's meant to say Susan. There are folded clothes, it looks like a pink jumper and two pairs of socks turned into balls. White socks, long ones, they must be for me. I've been praying for white socks, I'm sick of getting teased for wearing my brother's old grey ones. My heart thumps in my chest. I know I shouldn't be here, shouldn't be looking. There's been some kind of mistake. It isn't Christmas for another two days. I swallow down the lump in my throat and shut the door.

On the kitchen table, the toast rack's empty, but the cereal box is open. Yesterday Paul found the plastic toy but he didn't eat any Krispies. I told Mummy it wasn't fair, you've got to eat the cereal to get the prize, but she said not to fuss and that life's not fair. Mummy's sitting on a stool reading over by the oven and the door's wide open, making the room warm. The washing's hanging from the ceiling on something called a Sheila's maid. I'm glad it's not called a Susan's maid. Mist covers the windows and I draw a flower to decorate the space, drips running down my finger.

'Time for breakfast.' Mummy closes the book. 'Go and get Paul. Tell him to come down right away.'

In our room, my bed is against the short wall, and Paul's is against the long wall. At night, light peeps through the slit in the curtains and I can see him. Sometimes we whisper to each other, if he's awake and I'm awake. If there's a row going on downstairs you can't sleep through that. Mummy says it's the drink that makes Daddy shout and when that happens I curl up like a snail, pull the covers around my neck and stare into space. I like to know where my knees and my legs are, it doesn't do to spread. You don't keep warm when you spread.

Paul jumps into his slippers now that there's food to be had. He rushes downstairs still reading his comic. I don't know how he does that without bumping into something. The door to the lounge is still closed, but Paul doesn't notice anything strange. I'm sorry that I looked in there now. Mummy says when you've done something wrong it's best to own up but I'm not so sure. I usually keep quiet but this makes Daddy angry and he shakes his fist. When I cry Mummy hugs me and then she sends me off to bed with a prod. It's strange going to bed in the middle of the day.

In my bowl is a mountain of Krispies and a moat of milk. I pour sugar from the shaker because I like a thick crust on top. Grandma hisses whenever she sees how much sugar I take but Mummy says I've got a sweet tooth, just like her. Paul's still reading the comic, and the pages shake when he laughs and his shoulders go up and down. Swinging my legs, I tap the tiles on the floor and try not to hit the cracks. The flower I drew on the window has disappeared into a stripy mess.

I finish my breakfast and I look around for Mummy but she's not in the kitchen. I slosh my empty dish around in the washing-up water and lean across the sink to reach for the mop with the shaggy head. Once I've finished, I turn the bowl upside down on the draining board. I rub the spoon and check it's clean by staring into the shiny bit. In the reflection, I see my cheeks are puffed like a gerbil's, and my fringe covers my eyes.

'You're looking at yourself again,' says Paul.

'No.' I put the spoon in the cutlery drawer.

Mummy rushes into the room, the flares on her trousers flapping. I wish I had a trouser suit like that. It's purple with a tunic that goes right up to her neck. Daddy ordered it from the catalogue especially for Christmas, but he's let her wear it a few times already.

'Have either of you been in the lounge this morning?' Mummy holds her forehead in her hand.

'Not yet,' says Paul. 'But I want to watch the telly later.'

I squeeze the dishcloth and the droplets splatter.

'What about you Susan?' I get busy cleaning up. 'Have you been into the front room?'

'No.' I stare at the taps when I answer.

'That's good,' she says. 'Just give me a few minutes, then you can watch telly all day if you want to. Special treat for Christmas.'

'Yippee,' says Paul.

'Oh.' I wonder what has happened to all the special things on the floor.

'You better get dressed,' says Mummy.

The lounge door's open when we come back downstairs and everything's tidy. The curtains are open and the lights on the tree flash. But there are no clothes, no white socks anywhere. They've gone, they've vanished. I wonder if I've spoilt our Christmas and that they'll be no presents for anyone. Perhaps it's my fault. I walk up the stairs, tears dripping from my eyes. Beside my pillow I find Ted-Ted, we sit on the floor and I squeeze him so tight that I can't breathe.

Daddy's in a good mood when he gets home. He says he's only got one more day to work until he has a well-earned rest. Hugging Mummy, he tucks his neck onto her shoulder and he

9

dances with her, shuffling from side to side. She giggles, his whiskers are tickling, she says. They cuddle for a bit, then Daddy sees me watching, and he lets go of Mummy. They stand holding hands, like they're going to play ring-a-ring-a-roses.

'I've got more good news for you, Alan,' Mummy says. 'A card arrived from my mother today.' She nods towards the one with three camels on it. Daddy walks to the mantelpiece. He doesn't even look at the picture, he's more interested in the piece of paper that falls out. 'D'you think that's enough to pay for everything?' Daddy nods and puts the paper in his wallet. 'It's a relief, isn't it? Now we can enjoy Christmas without worrying.'

On Christmas morning, we're not allowed out of our room until it's seven o'clock. Paul's in charge of the time, and I have to wait until he says it's okay to look for our presents. I wait in my bed while Paul chatters about the Scalextric set he hopes he'll get. Maybe I imagined seeing the room all covered with papers and the presents. Perhaps it was a dream. My heart pumps when Paul shouts and we race along the passage.

'Wow!' he says. 'There's a great big box under the tree. I bet that's for me.'

Mummy and Daddy follow us into the lounge. We can open the gifts from Father Christmas, but not the ones under the tree. Not yet, anyway. Mummy passes me a pink pillowcase and Paul has the blue one. There are lots of lumpy things inside, and I pull out the basket first. The red letters say 'Susan', that's better.

'What's this for?' Paul takes his out.

'It's a waste-paper basket,' says Mummy. 'Not many children have their own, personalised waste-paper basket. You can put your rubbish in there like drawings that you don't want anymore or sweet wrappers.'

'That'll be useful,' says Paul.

Inside my basket there's another present, tied with ribbon. I undo the bow and the paper falls open. I see the socks, the same ones from the other day, long and white.

'Do you like them?' asks Mummy.

'Yes.' I cross my arms and hold them next to my heart. 'They're just what I wanted.'

'Funny how Father Christmas always knows what you want,' says Mummy. Daddy's laughing and coughing at the same time. She gives him a little tap on the wrist and he becomes quiet. I open another present, and there's my pink jumper. I'm pleased and confused. Nothing's a surprise.

'What's up?' says Mummy. 'You look sad.'

'She's always been ungrateful, that little cow,' says Daddy.

I feel the tears coming and Mummy strokes my cheek.

'Whatever's the matter?' she asks.

'Nothing,' I gulp. 'But are you sure all these things come from Father Christmas?'

Camariñas

Sunshine leaks through a gauze of cloud and patches of sapphire appear. Dan parks the Mini Traveller beside a stream and we amble past the dunes. By the shore, water circles my ankles and I jump the waves as they turn. The tail of my cotton belt flies in the wind and I taste the salty stands of my hair. I cuff Dan's shoulder and he grabs my hand, dragging me along the beach while I whoop. We find a sheltered spot and sink onto the sand, waiting for the afternoon to meld into dusk.

When we return to the car, the stream has turned into a river. Fumes choke from the exhaust and the Mini Traveller splutters across. It dawdles along the road, burping and groaning, then like a naughty toddler, it refuses to move further. Dan lifts the bonnet and peers inside. I watch Dan and dither, wondering how to help. Opposite there's a row of shops and a man calls from a doorway in Spanish but I can't reply. I shrug and beckon him over. His smile crinkles the parched skin around his cheeks and he offers Dan a hand. The man stares at the engine then pulls free an octopus of wires and strikes a disposable lighter to dry the cover. Dan follows the man's gestures and gets inside the car. When he tries the engine it roars and Dan pokes his head through the open window to shout his thanks.

I catch my last breath of Camariñas. Already it is growing late and darkness hides the sea. But still I hear the waves, the rush of water on the soaked beach.

'Do we have to go?' I ask.

'Come on.' Dan fixes me with his caramel eyes. 'We'll find the hotel.'

Greenhayes

'Christ, what was that?' Frank doesn't answer but turns over, pulling the duvet with him. I roll out of bed and peek through the blinds. 'Sounded like a car backfiring.'

'Not on Greenhayes. There aren't any old bangers around here.'

I scan the cul-de-sac, looking for any sign of movement but it's all quiet. The mock-Tudor houses stand in a line and our bay window offers a good view. I notice movement on the porch next door. It would be a foolish burglar trying to gain entry at the front. Reaching for my glasses, I see more clearly. There's a naked woman slumped on the doormat. Her tapered legs stretch to the step and her skin's all pearly in the moonlight.

'Well I never!' I exclaim. The woman clasps her knees, trying to hide her breasts the size of honeydews. 'It's Jenny. Herman must've chucked her out.'

'I knew that marriage was never going to last.'

'But it's the middle of the night and she's got nothing on.' I grab Frank's dressing gown and I'm swamped in velvet while I search for the other robe.

'Blimey, what a woman.' Frank's at the window now he knows there's something worth watching. I stand beside him and we see Jenny shivering. 'You can't go interfering.'

'I'm only going to lend her my robe.'

'Herman went off his head when I cut a few inches off his precious Leylandii. You don't want to make an enemy of him.'

'I can't leave Jenny stuck on the porch like that. I'll never get a wink of sleep if I don't help her.'

I leave the house, my slippers clip-clopping as I walk to the boundary. The night is clear but the air clings. Standing on tiptoe I peer over the wall. She sees me and scurries through the shrubs. Passing over the robe I notice her fingers are like ice. She pulls a smile but looks set to burst into tears.

'Thank you.' Jenny's swollen top lip makes it hard for her to speak.

'Might stop you getting a cold – I'd invite you back but Frank says no. Won't hear of it after that last row he had with Herman.'

'It's okay.' She struggles to get her arms into the sleeves. 'Herman will let me in soon.'

'Okay then.'

I still can't sleep in spite of my good deed and when it's time to get up, I'm like a dish-rag. Limping to the window, I draw the blinds and there's no sign of Jenny. She must've found refuge somewhere. When I get downstairs, there's a parcel on the back porch. I peel back the brown paper and there's my robe all fluffy and warm from the tumble dryer. There was no need to wash and return it so promptly. I find an envelope nestling by the collar and inside there's a thank you note from Jenny. She's signed her name in loopy handwriting and at the bottom there's a smiley face. Only this smiley face has a black eye. I wonder if it's a coded message for help and I think about Jenny trapped in Herman's executive home like a modern-day Cinderella but without a prince in sight. I look again at the smiley face and decide it's not a black eye just a blot from the ballpoint pen.

Boy on the Beach

I bump the kerb as I reverse into a space, the only one left by the beach. My forehead's beaded with sweat and clumps of hair hang in damp strands. I tell the children to get out – Alexia and Beth hold hands as only best friends do and Tommy sucks his thumb. Jen's unpacking the boot and I go to help, the children have bags to carry and I give the picnic blanket to Tommy. Threading my arms through the straps of the backpack, I reach for the cool-box and Jen guides the children across the road.

'Keep your shoes on,' I warn the girls. 'You don't want the sand to burn your feet.' Alexia's weighed down by the bag she's looped over her shoulder and Beth walks exactly as her mother does, copying Jen's long strides. We cross the beach quickly, then we pick a path around the families already pitched by the shore.

'Here'll do,' Jen decides, throwing down the beach bag. I drop onto the sand. The girls have already set to work with their spades, their skirts tucked into their knickers. Thomas sits by me and watches. Scattering sand as she lays the blanket, Jen secures the corners by weighting them with books, shoes and sun cream. I move a little closer, conscious to give sufficient space to the neighbouring families. They talk in French and I guess they're looking down on us and our shambolic camp.

Slipping handfuls of sand through my fingers, I study the sea: flurries of white in the distance and ripples of cobalt and aqua. A breeze flaps my fringe and sends tickles across my arms. Already I'm picking up colour, a stripe shows where my watch should be; I've put it into my pocket, in case I go swimming. Thomas is ready for the beach, lathered with cream and dressed in his trunks. He watches the gulls circle around the diving platform, a tower poking out of the sea like the mast of a ship.

'I swim out there.' He points.

'No, Tommy. It's too far. You go for a paddle, but stay near the edge.' He skips across the sand to join the other children who are larking and jumping over the waves. I notice Alexia's nose is turning pink, and I call her over. She sits between my legs while I spread sun cream over, covering the dark moles on her neck thickly. I watch Thomas intermittently, his white hair like a beacon amongst the tanned flesh and costumes. This feels like a real holiday, somewhere different and exciting, away from the husbands that work in the city.

'All done.' I release her.

'Where's Tommy?' she asks.

'He's playing in the shallows.'

I look up, my finger poised to point in his direction and I study the bathers, their arms and legs like a thicket. In my peripheral vision I notice a boy and turn, but it's not Thomas. Flicking my head from side to side, my heart pumps. Alexia jumps to her feet and runs around in a circle, waving her arms in panic. I get up and shield my eyes from the sun then walk towards the sea. The slap of the waves and the shouting bathers annoy me now. I hurry back to the camp and find Jen laid out, her stomach sucked in, her ribs glistening.

'You're in my sun.' She speaks with her eyes closed.

'I can't find Thomas.'

'Isn't he with the girls?'

'No,' my voice quavers. Jen sits up, dusting sand from her palms.

'Take a walk along to the breaker, see if he's with the children paddling over there.'

'Okay. Will you watch Alexia? I don't want to lose both children.'

'He's not lost, Gina. He's just playing.' She leans back onto her elbows and glances around.

'Will you watch Alexia?' I say again.

'If you want.' She re-ties the laces of her halter neck, her eyes fixed on the blanket.

I pass the girls: Alexia is hopping like a demented chicken and Beth hangs onto an arm, anchoring her.

'Stay here.' I tell Alexia. 'I'm going to find Tommy.'

'Tommy's lost!' she says.

'It's all right,' I say, but I don't see her, I see the blur of a child in panic. 'Mummy will find him.'

I walk to where the seawater gathers in a lagoon. Big boys paddle to their knees and wield fishing nets. A discarded crisp packet swirls in the water and there's a smell of debris. I crinkle my nose and squint. School-aged girls kick the waves, splashing each other. There's no sign of Thomas. I think about calling his name, but there are too many screaming children and squawking gulls to make my voice heard. My mouth's dry and I press my hand against my forehead.

Gathering pace as I walk back to Jen, I crumple onto the blanket, out of breath. I swallow my anxiety, tears spilling from the corners of my eyes.

'Don't worry,' says Jen. 'There's a tannoy system – see the speakers lined along the path? I'll find out where lost children are sent.' She puts on a T-shirt and straightens her shorts.

'Hurry,' I say. 'Please.'

'I'm calling to mind my 'A' level French. Glad it'll finally be useful.'

Jen takes a path around the crowds to reach a wooden shelter. She talks to a man sitting at a table, she nods and points. My pounding heart makes my whole body jerk and Alexia's pleading at my side. I wait. A ping-pong tune from the speakers quiets the beach. Everyone is still, listening to the crackle that shows the microphone's working. When the announcement comes, somehow I understand the French. A little English boy's lost, three-years-old, blonde, wearing blue trunks, his name's Thomas. Please alert the office if you see him. A final ping-pong and the holiday-makers resume their conversations. From behind me I hear a woman speak: why is it the English who always lose their children? Jen returns, hands in her pockets.

'Has he shown up yet?' she asks.

'No. No sign of him. What do I do now?'

'No-one's going to let him drown on a beach this busy.'

'It's not drowning I'm worried about,' I squeal. 'Maybe he's been abducted.'

'Ducted?' Alexia repeats. I hold her hands, her expression reflects the fear I sense and I have to convince her that everything's going to be fine.

'I'm going to walk along the beach and find him. You wait here with Jen and Beth. I'll be back in no time, and then we'll have ice-cream.'

'Okay.' Her round eyes show she trusts me.

17

I walk by the edge of the water where the wet sand clings to my toes. There's urgency in my limbs but my mind's foggy. I call Tommy's name and gasp, then I cough and try again. Swinging my arms, I take long steps, my shadow surging forwards. I think of Steve sitting at his desk, away from the mayhem. He never wanted me to take this holiday and now he'll kill me if I can't find Tommy. I cast my head from side to side, hoping I'll spot him in the distance. I'm crying and calling, scanning the faces on the beach, all of them realising I'm the careless mother. The crowds begin to thin and there are fewer bathers in the water but the beach stretches further. Like a mirage, fuzzy at the edges, I see my boy jumping the shallows, chasing the waves. It's him, it's absolutely him: fluffy white hair, sturdy legs, blue patterned trunks. I run to him and collapse in the water.

'Tommy, Tommy. What are you doing?'

'Jumping,' he says. My fingers grip him like pincers and I hug him to me. The water circles us. 'Row the boat, Mummy,' he says. 'Row, row, row the boat.' He struggles free and finds my hands, tugging my arms like oars. Dropping my head to hide my tears, I join the game. Thomas sings and giggles, I mumble out-of-tune. As soon as the verse is over, I drag Tommy's arm to make him stand.

'Come on,' I say. 'Alexia's worried. You've been missing for ages.'

'I been playing.'

'I know, but let's get back.'

Thomas raises his arms, wanting to be carried. I lift him, glad of his weight, his legs wrap around my waist, his head tucks under my chin. I hear him chewing his thumb and his saliva drips onto my collarbone. My knees shake as I walk, my feet sinking into the sand. Anonymous faces watch my progress then a man approaches.

'Is this the missing boy?' His English is good.

'Yes, thank God I found him.'

'I saw him in the water and I went to ask him if his name was Thomas but he said no and carried on playing.'

'Oh,' I say. 'Thank you for trying.' He nods and I struggle on. The child wriggles in my arms, the boy who only knows himself as Tommy.

Six-word Story

Missing: Chloe's heart,
                    lost in transit.

Hitching

Sieving dry earth through my fingers, I make little towers that crumble immediately. Sweat trickles down my spine and I brush needles of grass from my jeans. Staring into the distance, the Outback reminds me of a lumpy picnic blanket with yellow-green tufts. It's not much to look at but at least the days of pavements and puddles are over. Sliding a mirror from my backpack, I notice my cheeks are pink and I smooth sunscreen over.

'Have you got any lip gloss?' I ask.

Jane looks up from the magazine and fishes in her pocket.

'Catch.' She lobs a small tube and then returns to her reading, pinching the pages that have flipped over in the breeze.

'Perhaps we should've caught the Greyhound.'

'We can always do that tomorrow, if we don't get a ride today.'

When the sun casts a honey-glaze on the land, a road train approaches. Squealing brakes bring it to a stop and I stand beside the second of two huge containers, each set on dozens of wheels, all taller than Jane. The cab door opens and the truckie leans out, waving a hand blotchy with tattoos.

'You girls shouldn't be hitching,' he shouts. 'The Territory's a wild place. It's only safe to take a lift from a truckie. Where yous heading?'

'Darwin,' I splutter.

'You're in luck – get in.'

Jane nods, dark curls tumbling into her eyes, and I take the cue, climbing the treads. The cab is roomier than I expect: a bench set back from the windscreen, the steering wheel sprouting from the middle of the floor. I push sweet wrappers and old newspapers away, making space on the seat.

'Too right.' The truckie speaks from the corner of his mouth. 'Make yourself at home.' He slaps the bench indicating where I should sit and Jane settles at the end.

'What d'they call yous?'

'I'm Claire and this is Jane. Thank you for stopping.'

'No worries. Poms are yous? I'm Graham.'

21

'Good to meet you,' I say, but I forget his name at once.

Air rushes through the driver's window and a fan pulses but the atmosphere is stuffy. Besides the odd grunt, the truckie doesn't say very much and I struggle to keep the conversation going.

'Hey you. What's yer name? Jan is it?'

'Jane.'

'You want to take a sleep in the back?' He nods in the direction of the bunk behind and Jane peers into the space. Throwing aside a T-shirt that smells of diesel, she scrambles inside.

'Right!' The truckie slaps my thigh, clawing the denim with his jagged nails. When he removes his hand to change gears, I wriggle away and shift my bag from the floor, wedging it between us to prevent further contact. He looks at my new position and laughs.

Through the windscreen opaque with dust, I trace the road as it slices the land. Decaying kangaroo carcasses mark the route like milestones, victims of road kill. I turn and watch the truckie as he rolls a cigarette, the paper and tobacco balanced on his knee. The radio hums as if creatures from outer space are trying to make contact. The truckie coughs and tosses me a small container that rattles with pills.

'Smoking's a killer,' he says. 'Try some speed.'

I fiddle with the lid and shake a pill into my palm.

'One's not enough – pass them to me!' Upending the container against his mouth, I hear the drugs tumble and as the truckie crunches, speckles of white pattern his face. He throws the pill bottle back towards me and I'm conscious of him watching as I shake out another tablet. Aiming one and then the other at the back of my throat, I swallow. What the hell – it's going to be a long journey.

The road becomes like a mesmerising snake as it shimmies into the retreating distance. I lose track of time as my eyeballs roll and my chin bounces against my chest. My mouth falls open only to be clamped shut when my eyes ping into focus. When it's dark the truckie brings the road train to a stop and he jumps to the ground. I listen for his footsteps as he wanders into the night. Peering through the glass, a swollen moon shows his silhouette walking away.

'I'm beginning to regret this.'

'Too late now.' Jane slithers from the bunk onto the seat next to me. We rest our foreheads together, our clammy skin sticks. Taking turns, we look over the dashboard. He's out there, whimpering and thrashing around. Smoothing a lock of hair between my fingers I suck the ends.

Pummelling and scraping sounds interrupt my trance-like state. Jutting forwards, I see a mass of dark hides turning the earth black. Like floodwater, the cattle spill across the land, their heads nodding up and down like mechanical toys. The truckie jumps and swings his arms, a matchstick figure weaving between the herd. Once he's free, he recovers his power. This time he gives a rasping shout, and, through the barren landscape, he strides towards the truck.

Leaping onto the metal ladder, the crashing footfalls announce his progress. He pants as he works his way upwards, and with each step I shrink a little smaller. The cab tilts as he balances his weight, and he tugs on the door but it doesn't swing free. Instead, he lurches on top of the engine, sprawling in front of us, the windscreen our only protection. He levels his bloodshot eyes and mouths incomprehensible words. Grappling with the wipers, he gets to his knees then he surges onto the roof of the cab. Kettledrum beats echo while he dances. My breathing shallows as the fear creeps. I count his footsteps until the pace slows and I guess the roof will hold his weight while the truckie sleeps. Jane ducks her head as if the truckie's pressing her down and my neck feels short with my shoulders all tense. I look towards Jane – our eyes meet then part again, meet then part again – until I'm consumed by sleep.

Coming to consciousness, my eyelids flicker and daylight shoots through the cab as the driver's door jerks open. I feign sleep as the night-time memories invade. The truckie whistles as he moves around the cab. Jane's body is warm next to mine and I brave a glimpse through slit eyes. The truckie's searching for something wedged by the door.

'G'day,' he says and aiming the aerosol of deodorant, he sprays.

Your Life

'Your life'll be unrecognisable in a few hours,' the midwife smiled. Kirsty sucked on the mouthpiece, the gas and air made her eyes dilate. Damp hair framed her face and her cheeks were flushed.

'No it won't.' Ben tossed the golfing magazine onto the bed and paced around the room. 'The baby'll fit into our lifestyle.'

'You might find that difficult.' The midwife read her watch as she took Kirsty's pulse. 'Babies don't come to order. Yours may not sleep, the baby might be a reluctant feeder or plagued by colic.'

'I doubt it.' Ben opened the overnight bag which was stuffed with scented candles, massage oil, and world music CDs. He dug to the bottom and pulled out a zip-bag containing nuts. Tucking into the almonds, he realised he'd missed breakfast in the rush to reach the hospital and already it was past lunchtime. He made an excuse to slip out of the room, then headed for the canteen.

Kirsty was dozing when he returned so he sat in the armchair. The broadsheet rustled as he folded the pages and she opened her eyes.

'They've given me an epidural to help with the pain,' she said.

'You're doing brilliantly.' Ben took her hand and traced the lines on her palm with his finger. 'I'm so proud of you. I love you, darling.'

'You'll love me even more when I give you a son.'

'Indeed,' said Ben. 'Only make it quick, there's a drinks party starting at six.'

Beginners' Guide

Hold the newborn in the crook of your arm and release your breast. Jab the nipple into the infant's mouth. If the child is not ready to feed, it may not open its mouth. In this case, press a finger on the baby's chin and wait for the lips to pucker. Make sure the infant attaches properly. Where 'latch-on' occurs, the vacuum seals to ensure correct feeding. In cases where 'latch-on' fails, cracked nipples or seepage may result. Compensation for damage to breasts is only available to mothers who ensure that 'latch-on' is successful. A supporting letter from a midwife may be required as evidence in a claim.

Once the child has begun to feed, it is important that he or she receives the correct dose of milk. Do not let the infant fall asleep during feeding. It is natural for the child to appear drowsy but steps should be taken to ensure wakefulness. Try prodding the cheek or tickling the neck. When feeding has finished, remember to wipe the nipple with a damp cloth. The baby may require winding following breastfeeding. This can be achieved by holding the child in one hand and stroking its back with the other (a circular action is frequently effective). Alternatively, you may prefer to use a tapping or patting movement. When a burp is sounded, the process is complete.

Take care of your breasts and they will provide excellent feeding and service, birth after birth. There are no known side effects to breastfeeding, but if you experience your mood or mental health deteriorating, please contact a doctor immediately. Remember to continue feeding your child — formula preparations are not recommended.

Bread

The baker cuts chunks from the amoeba dough that's spreading across the counter. It is sticky in his hands, protesting against its separation onto the kneading board. By the till there's a display of loaves, shiny like glazed pots. I grip the largest and pass it to the assistant who swaddles it in tissue. I carry the bread like a babe in my arms, its heat warming my bones as I walk back home.

Collusion

Vera rang the doorbell then waited in the drizzle. With a finger she wiped dirt from the edge of the window frame then wondered what to do with her hand, now that it was marked. There was no point in searching her handbag again for the key. She knew where it was, hanging with the others on the rack in the hall and forgotten in her hurry to leave the house. There was nothing for it but to wait for Reg to answer the door. He was bound to be inside, it's not as if he had the strength or enthusiasm for an outing these days, and especially not in the rain. Ellen threaded her arm through the crook of Vera's elbow, and she grinned at Vera's surprise.

'I've always startled easily, even as a child,' said Vera. 'It must have something to do with being evacuated. I've never got over that feeling of being abandoned.'

'You've told me that before, Grandma.'

'Some memories never leave you alone.'

'I guess not.'

It was good to feel Ellen's warmth, to have the body contact that had become so rare now that the grandchildren had grown up. Friends and relatives kept their distance but for a cursory kiss and Reg had long since given up the habit of hugging. Vera tapped her foot, watching the water splash on the patent leather court shoes. She'd dressed up for the occasion, it wasn't often that she was taken out to lunch. Not to the posh place at the top of town, where they served nibbles before the starter for free. Ellen was more used to these things than Vera had ever been. The early bird menu at the local steak house was more Reg's style.

Eating out with Reg was more trial than pleasure but she suffered it for the sake of having a night off from cooking the evening meal. She knew all too well that he'd click his fingers to gain attention but at least he'd stopped calling the waiters 'Pancho'. The advent of political correctness had at last reached the depths of Reg's consciousness. Either that or her tutting had finally made a difference. When the meal arrived, he'd pick at the meat, complain about the gristle and leave the debris of food under the napkin because his appetite wasn't up to a man-size meal. He'd make a show of paying the bill, and leave a reasonable tip to confirm his elevated status over those who served him.

'I'll try knocking on the window. Maybe he'll hear that. He's probably dozed off in front of the television.'

'Try the bell again first.' Ellen pushed the button and the chimes rang out.

'Don't ring it too many times. That'll only make him bad tempered.'

'That's nothing new,' sniggered Ellen. Vera gave a half-hearted smile.

When the rain fell more heavily, Ellen took her umbrella from the oversized handbag and they stood together, listening to the scattering of droplets under its shelter. Vera felt a fool, standing there, helpless. She hoped none of the neighbours would realise she was locked out. Running her fingers through the damp ends of her hair, she guessed the work of the hairdresser would be ruined. It wasn't often that she treated herself to a blow-dry but she needed the cut anyway.

Reg's outline appeared spiky behind the obscured panel in the door. He'd not bothered to put his clothes on, the corduroy collar of his dressing gown like a shroud against his pale skin. Vera pushed the door as he released the latch and it rebounded against his foot as he stood motionless in the entrance.

'Are you not feeling well?' Vera recognised the whisky fumes but ploughed on, hoping Ellen wouldn't notice. 'Did you go back to bed? Is that why it took you so long to answer the door?' He stepped back and faltered on ankles not stable enough to support him. 'You better get back upstairs. You don't want to be spreading germs, do you?' Vera took his arm, but he fought her off by extending a finger and jabbing her on the shoulder. Sensing Ellen was behind her in the doorway, she ushered Reg into the corner and turned her face to speak. 'You go through to the back room, Ellen. I'll get your Granddad upstairs.'

'Can I help?' Ellen squeezed past.

'You can fuck off,' said Reg. 'We don't need you coming round here and flaunting your money. You're just a kid. If you think you're going to get the better of me, you've got another think coming.'

Ellen threaded the handle of her bag between clenched fists, her knuckles white, and she studied the wooden block flooring.

'It's all right, Ellen, Granddad's had one too many, it seems.'

'I'm pissed,' he said. 'And it serves you right.'

'He's not getting at you, Ellen. Just go inside and wait for me there.'

'I thought you weren't coming back for another hour. I'd have sobered up by then if you'd kept to time.'

'Let's not worry about that now. I'll help you upstairs and you can sleep it off.'

Ellen was sat on the footstool clutching her knees. She looked like a little girl with wisps of hair around her forehead and a lock hanging over her eye. Collected on the table were the empties, the bottles like a silhouette of city skyscrapers. It was funny how Reg was neat and tidy in his drinking, but not so careful with his language or gestures. He'd cursed Ellen all the way up the stairs. Poor girl. It's not as if she'd done anything wrong. She was just unfortunate to have Reg as a grandfather.

'He's only like that because of the drink.' Vera put her arm around Ellen's shoulder. 'He doesn't mean anything by it.'

'Of course not.' Ellen wiped away the tear that streaked her cheek.

Keeping Quiet

The guests gathered on the terrace to see the newlyweds off, and Sally fussed about her dress. She'd ripped the apricot trim when she'd trod on the hem and the bodice was ill-fitting since she'd lost all the weight. Of course it was Miranda who caught the bouquet, and she lifted it like an Olympic torch, then flashed a fuchsia smile in Sally's direction. Ignoring her, Sally waved as the car crunched along the gravel drive all the way to the gatehouse. Rod unbuttoned his collar and tucked the cravat into his pocket.

'I fixed the car with a kipper under the bonnet, put it right by the air vents,' he said.

'Very inventive.' Sally blew the stray strands of her fringe away from her face. 'Your speech was…entertaining.'

'Yeah.' Rod necked the remaining champagne from a glass abandoned on a table. 'I'll bring the car round to the front, then I'll say goodbye to Miranda. Can you be ready in ten minutes?'

'Fine.' She watched him swagger away in the morning suit, imagined the conceited smirk on his face.

Sally collected the holdall from her room and Rod slung it in the boot. She shuddered as he took the driver's seat and the silence between them pricked. She fiddled with the buttons on the CD player, then turned it off.

'When shall we tell them?' asked Sally. 'We can't keep delaying. We'll need to say something before they start showing the photographs.'

'After they're back from honeymoon. That's the right time.'

'It's been a dreadful day. The way they kept going on about following the example of their best man and bridesmaid.' Sally frowned. 'Will you collect your stuff by the end of the week?'

'If that's okay,' said Rod.

'Yes, and I'll instruct a solicitor.'

Quiz

Change the final diary entry in this real-life sequence (see 'Saturday' below), so that married life for Gail Aldwin begins on a more positive note. *In Lurve* reader, Gail says, 'I've never got over the loss of my wedding ring. A ring is an important symbol of true and everlasting love. Please make it possible for me to re-imagine events and give me a start to married life that I'll be happy to remember.'

Wednesday
Jon found my Dad's number in the telephone directory. He told me he was going to do things properly or not at all. The service might be booked but he'd need my father's permission to marry me. I knew he had no credit on his mobile so when I saw him in the phone box I guessed he'd reversed the charges. I managed to have a word with Dad once I'd wrestled the receiver from Jon. Dad said I was to be congratulated, Jon sounded like a decent bloke and as long as I was happy, that was the main thing.

Thursday
Jon told an old woman buying bread from the market that we were two people who were so in love that we had to get married at once. The only thing stopping us was the need for a ring. Didn't she have enough gold bands on her wedding finger to let one go spare? We watched while she tugged the ring, licking her knuckle to ease it free. She said it was all right, that she still had the others, and she handed the tarnished band over. She was glad, she said, to help a man who truly knew the meaning of love.

Friday
The registrar suggested that Jon ask the cleaner and his wife to be the witnesses. She said I looked pretty in my blouse. Jon had been in an argument earlier that morning (although it wasn't his fault) and his wedding shirt was sprayed with droplets from the punch that caught him on the nose. We said the words, signed our names, and I wore the ring. Afterwards we went to the pub

for a drink and celebrated our whirlwind romance. There aren't many people who meet at a bus stop and fall in love.

Saturday

We drank coffee from polystyrene cups at the bus station, nursing our hangovers. I lost the wedding ring sometime during the night – must've slipped off my finger, it was too big anyway. Jon was angry and shouted when he found out. Then he said it didn't matter, that he was the eternal optimist and something else would turn up. We'd have more luck in the next town.

Social Surfing

Placing the lilies in the centre of the table, Vik thought the pink petals curled like tongues and she noticed the perfume drifting. The stamens were well away from the napkins folded into crowns, she didn't want the linen to be marked, at least not before the dinner guests arrived. Taking a step back, she admired the table: the crystal glasses blinked as sunshine leaked through the patio windows, the cutlery was laid in orderly rows, the place-cards were adorned with italic script indicating where each guest should sit. Vik had gambled on the best people to invite, keen to get into the group of parents at the playground gate. It was no fun standing alone while others chatted. Andy and Trudy lived a few doors away, so that was another reason to ingratiate. Ellen and Stuart shared the care of Lewis, the boy Damian gravitated towards each morning at drop off. Damian skipped around him, tapped his shoulder and smiled at the blonde boy.

Vik had selected dishes that could be made in advance, and a casserole was simmering in the oven. Raw beef was sliced in the fridge, ready to make carpaccio, and the apple pie with its lattice top was cooling in the dish. Serving bread and dripping was an after-thought but one that would go down well with the men, judging by the way Simon lapped it up, like mother's milk. It was a small reminder of home, her father's restaurant in the mountains, where bread was served with a smothering, to soak up the beer.

She wore a silk dress, the fabric drawn in at the waist to accentuate her shape. Simon went casual with an open-neck shirt. Damian was occupied by the playstation, moved to his bedroom as a treat and for the purpose of keeping him upstairs. Vik studied her fingernails and admired the glittering shine that complemented the lilac outfit. Arranging the bottles, Simon offered her a drink but she preferred to wait until the guests arrived. When the doorbell rang she walked into the hall and swung the door open to greet the two couples who had arrived simultaneously.

In the lounge, the women shared the sofa while the men stood drinking whisky. Vik brought through a dish piled with smoked salmon on brown slices, and, alongside, the dripping glistened on country bread. Ellen asked about the choice and accepted the smoked salmon. Trudy disguised a sneer and did likewise. It was okay, she'd made the dripping for the men anyway. Andy's eyes bulged as he studied the plate, taking the largest serving of bread and dripping.

'In my day, we'd pile a load of salt on top.' He took a bite. 'But I see you've already done that for us.'

'It's traditional to serve it like this,' boasted Simon. 'Vik grates up the lard, seasons it, then rolls it into balls for spreading.'

'My word,' said Stuart. 'It was always a treat to have bread and dripping at my grandmother's house.'

'That's because she was as poor as a church mouse,' sniped Ellen. 'Couldn't afford anything better.'

'Have some more smoked salmon.' Vik turned the plate towards the women, anxious to scotch the idea that she was impecunious. 'Men seem to love rustic flavours, but it's not to everyone's taste.'

'Reminds me of when I studied in Spain. I had an elderly neighbour and baked an apple and blackberry pie for a treat. As soon as she saw the berries she pushed the plate away. Said it reminded her of Franco and the days when she foraged for food to save from starving.' Trudy nibbled the flaky edge of salmon.

'So you're a linguist like Vik, are you?' Simon enquired.

'I took joint honours in French and Spanish,' said Trudy. 'What did you do, Vik?'

'I'm not nearly as well qualified but I do speak Polish.'

'I'd never have guessed – what happened to your accent?'

'Came over with EU accession, did you?' Andy joined the interrogation.

'Yes and no. My parents sent me here. They didn't want me to end up running the family business.'

'Can't speak highly enough of Polish builders,' said Stuart. 'Finished our kitchen extension in weeks and they had no qualms about being paid in cash.'

'And doughnuts,' scoffed Ellen.

'Yes, well,' said Simon trying to turn the conversation. 'Vik is very proud of her heritage. She's teaching Damian to speak Polish.'

'Spanish is the way to go,' Andy winked. 'Especially if you've an eye on the Latin American markets.'

'Or Mandarin,' Simon interjected. 'World's largest economy.'

'Stuff and nonsense,' Stuart jostled into the conversation. 'English is the mainstay for international trade.'

'Good job we're all fluent in that case,' said Vik.

'Perhaps we should go into the dining room if you're ready to eat.' Simon led the way. 'Vik's been busy all day.'

'A dinner party's such a lovely, old-fashioned idea.' Ellen inspected the table.

'Makes a change from a country supper.' Trudy took her place.

Winded by the barrage of barely disguised slights, Vik caught her breath in the kitchen. At least she would impress them with the starter: slivers of the best quality raw beef, nestled on a bed of leaves. The idea came from a lunch she'd had at a Jamie Oliver restaurant and no-one was likely to criticise a recipe from the man who heralded quality school meals. Ellen picked at the meat but ate the leaves, Trudy camouflaged her leftovers under the cutlery, the men wolfed theirs back. Clearing the plates, Vik gained a modicum of respect from the party.

The casserole steamed as she served it at the table. Simon brought through the vegetable bowls and refilled the wine glasses. She told them it was venison, and Andy joked that it was road-kill from an accident in Richmond Park. Vik let that one go, and smiled politely as she sat.

'Of course,' said Stuart. 'My grandmother wasn't beyond accepting a rabbit from a poacher and making a pie. Tasty stuff.'

'Don't say that within Lewis's hearing,' said Ellen. 'You know how he loves Little Rabbit Foo Foo.'

'So does Damian. Goes around bopping us on the head, just like in the story,' said Vik.

'You've got to come from poor stock to appreciate what's good in life, eh Vik?' said Stuart.

'We weren't exactly poor but we did live under a communist regime.'

'Precisely.' Stuart wiped his mouth, smearing gravy across the linen napkin. 'My mother was so poor that she sewed ribbon onto my Y fronts and passed them on to my sister as hand-me-downs.'

'I once lived for a week off a square of cheese I found at the back of the fridge in my student digs,' said Andy. 'Beat that.'

The room became quiet again except for Trudy's laboured breathing. 'I'm sorry, chaps, I'm going to have to pop out for a ciggie. You can hold the dessert until I get back, can't you, Vik? Or should I say pudding?'

'Say what you like,' said Vik. 'No-one's holding back. We've got apple pie so that should suit you fine because there are no blackberries.'

'Great,' said Trudy. 'You know I didn't mean to offend, or anything.'

'Of course not,' said Vik.

Vik tapped her fingers on the granite work-surface, counting the seconds until Trudy returned from the garden. Perhaps I can feign a headache, she thought, and leave Simon to cope. Or better still, I'll check on Damian and announce he's got a fever, that'll send them scurrying for fear of catching it. But none of the excuses seemed plausible and she was forced to continue the charade. They ate the dessert, drank the coffee, and tried the truffles that she had rolled in cocoa. Handmade, she told them and showed her palms. Ellen sniffed.

'Right,' said Vik. 'That's it for tonight. I'm sure you've got better things to do in the morning than suffer from a hangover.'

'I'm not so sure about that.' Stuart dribbled as he spoke, a line of saliva on his chin like a slug's trail. 'You and me, we've got a lot in common, eh Vik?'

'Besides our sons being the same age and in the same class?'

'That's enough to be getting on with,' said Ellen.

'And he can always come to our house for a play-date,' said Trudy.

So, the offers came tumbling in: a barbecue in the garden, neighbours drinks at Christmas, fortieth birthday parties in the future. Vik folded her napkin and, smoothing the fabric, she thought better of agreeing to anything.

Fish Pond

There's splashing in the fish pond when I put out the rubbish and I guess the frogs are at it again. I find a torch and shine it over. Some of them are riding piggy back like double-headed beasts. There's at least a dozen in there – that must make it an orgy. A toad sits on the edge, winking at me. His ungainly body becomes lithe when he springs into the water. I watch the activity like a voyeur, then I scuttle back to the kitchen.

In the morning, a Mallard observes the results of the night's activity. Standing on one leg, he cocks his silky jade head, then takes a stroll around the pond. When he quacks, the female descends, spread winged from the roof. She's like a babe in a bathtub, scooping through the weeds with her beak, throwing back her head to gobble spawn.

Baby Blues

Lining up the bottles of baby formula, I thank God for the respite of when she's asleep. An adult's company is a bonus, even if he's only come to fix the boiler. Alex raps his knuckles on the kitchen counter. The back of his hand is smattered with freckles and his skin has the honey shade of a light tan. 'I'll be back to do the service next year. Thanks for the cuppa.' He counts the notes that I offer and folds them.

'You mean I've got twelve months to wait until I see you again?' Tilting my head I notice his red hair is streaked with grey, rather more silver than gold. He smiles, making the dimples appear. I bite my lip, resisting the urge to smile back, and Alex lingers, the silence holding us. Moving closer, he angles his head to reach my lips. His bristles scrape as he works his tongue and I wrap my arms around his neck. When saliva seeps onto my chin, I nudge his elbow and step away. Studying the lines of laminate on the floor, I straighten my shirt.

'I can drop by one day next week.' Alex arranges the tools in his belt.

'That isn't such a good idea, there's the baby to think about.'

'And your husband, or is he a boyfriend?'

'She's my partner, actually.'

'You mean I just kissed a dyke?' He tosses the spanner in his hand and aims it at the window. Stepping back as the glass shatters, his blood speckles the paintwork. My shoulders cinch and I'm frozen in place. Slamming the door as he leaves, air seeps through the broken glass. I force my limbs to work, treading carefully to avoid the shards, and I stare through the jagged hole. Alex is on the pavement. He swings his head from side to side, as if he's checking for witnesses, and a few moments later the van drives away. I'm left wondering how to explain the damage, but the baby's still asleep, so I have time to plan.

Pudding

Grandma holds the dish using a tea towel to stop the rim from burning her fingers. Already on the table are the tinned apricots, turtles swimming in the syrup. She places the egg custard alongside and stops to admire her creation. The skin is creamy and dotted with nutmeg, bulging like the breast of a female thrush. My mouth waters as she searches for the serving spoon hidden beside the table mats. Grandpa drums a tune with his fingers on the table and wears his napkin like a bib, a blob of gravy still on his cheek. I'm ready for my pudding, the youngest always gets served first. Grandma scoops the apricots into a bowl then carves a corner of custard. She scrapes the burnt edge and flicks the ends on top.

'There you are.' She passes the bowl and I examine my portion.

'Can I have a bit more skin?'

'Askers don't get.' Grandma waves the spoon like she's conducting an orchestra.

'Don't ask, don't want.' Grandpa chips in.

'Honestly, George,' she slaps another dollop of custard into my bowl. 'You're incorrigible.'

Grandpa gives me a wink and I giggle. I wait with my spoon ready in my hand and when Grandma sits, the race for a second helping begins.

Sand

Deana's temples pulsed as she remembered staggering along the promenade, clinging to his sleeve. She tried to make him dance by twirling under his arm but he told her to stop messing about. The streetlights dodged around the midnight-sky and music belted through the open car windows that streamed past. She lost one of her sandals and walked barefoot, swinging the other by the strap. It was later that she lurched onto the sand as if belly flopping onto water. *I should never have tried to match him, drinking shorts indeed.* Rubbing her forehead, she struggled to remember the details and she wondered whether she'd been pushed. She lifted her top to search for bruises but all she saw was a suntanned stripe. *I must've tripped – I'm so clumsy – what an idiot.*

The tour bus was quiet, some of the passengers were still asleep in the bunks upstairs, the others had long since gone into town for food or amusement. Air funnelled through the lower deck, making an empty cigarette packet skid across the kitchen counter. Deana slouched in the booth. Propping an elbow on the table, she held her head. *If I were at home, I could shrug this off, I'd be unlikely to see him again. But this bus trip, this journey, has over a month to run.* Deana contemplated their destination, and images of desert watering holes came of mind. There was mystery about Morocco, somewhere she could lose herself and become another person.

Startled from her day-dreams by footsteps descending the stairs, Deana tensed. *Suppose that's him.* But she recognised Ian's mud-splattered jeans long before the rest of him appeared and she relaxed her shoulders.

'What you doing?' Ian called over.

'Nothing. I was thinking, you know.'

'Thinking about what?'

'About how much longer we'll be stranded here.'

'It won't be long. Mart's promised to get the engine fixed this afternoon and then we'll be on our way.'

'That's good. I can't wait to get out of France.'

'Me too. I've had enough of the Merlot – I want to try some Rioja.' Ian took a couple of paces into the kitchen and lifted the kettle from the stove, swinging it in the air to gauge the level of water. 'There's enough for a pot. D'you want a cuppa?'

'Yes, please.' She watched him search the overhead lockers where the rations were stored: a few tins of hot-dogs, some dried mashed potato sachets, a bag of flour. 'The tea's in the cupboard at this end.' Deana pointed above the sink.

'D'you take milk?' He pulled the lid off a container and peered inside. 'There's a spoonful of the dried, if you want.'

'No, weak and black's fine for me.'

The tea spilt as he slapped the mugs on the table. Deana grabbed a cloth and wiped the surface but the activity made her dizzy. She returned to the seat opposite Ian, her hand shaking as she lifted the mug.

'You all right?' Ian shot a frown.

'Yeah, I'm okay.'

He stared at the lines of checked fabric that upholstered the seat. Deana chased the grains of wood on the table with her fingernail. The silence palled. Deana concentrated her energy, willing Ian to speak.

'Hard to believe this bus served twenty years in the transport fleet before being refitted,' he said.

'Not much of a refit. These chairs have the same material as on the London buses.'

'I think they've done it pretty well, specially as travelling by double decker is the cheapest way to go.'

'You're right.' Silence again. Ian clicked his tongue and stared at the CDs stacked alongside the player on the shelf as if deciding which one to put on. Instead he got up, lingered for a moment, then turned and headed outside.

I think Ian knows. I wouldn't put it past Brett to blab it around. She imagined the talk. It's always the quiet ones who you'd least expect who put it about. Deana remembered laughing as she sprawled on the beach and tasted sand. She levered her body onto all fours, the damp night air clinging while the inky water slid. It was then that he pounced, yanking at her hips so that her knees ploughed a trail. Still she laughed. Only when he tore at her underwear, elastic scoring her thighs, did she realise what was to happen. He positioned her legs then rammed into her and she chewed her lips while the pumping continued. With her face flat against the sand, her shoulder took his weight, and her limbs jarred with each thrust. She counted the waves, watching the lacy froth furl. She listened for the rasp of his flies to confirm it was over. Then she fell on her side and curled like an ammonite, clasping her ankles and hoping, wishing, she was somewhere else.

Her lips were cracked, and when she pulled a tag of skin she winced. *That's not the worst of it, I could be pregnant.* She found her bag tucked between the seats and flapped her diary open. Searching for the right page, she counted the days and realised that her period should start soon, there'd be just a short sentence of reproach. Putting an asterisk in the margin she closed the book. *I must finish my tea, nurse my hangover and hope for the best.* But Deana's advice faltered when she remembered making a play for Brett that evening, hanging on his every word in the bar and then in the casino when she'd draped her arms over his shoulders while he played blackjack. *What an idiot.* She slung the dregs of her tea in the sink and filled the bowl to begin washing up. Bubbles skirted to the edges but there was enough water to clean her cup and the few dishes abandoned on the side. *How long can I avoid Brett? What will I say when we come face-to-face?* Lines of dialogue rippled through her mind and she practised the words, mouthing each one silently, as if a golf ball was balanced on her tongue. *You might've asked me for a shag, I'd have given it to you anyway.*

The sunshine enticed Deana outside. Curling leaves showed signs of autumn, and beyond the bamboo fence the horizon trimmed the length of sky. *I'm lucky to be away from London, the grey days and rain. I'm free with a whole bright future ahead.* She fished in her pocket for the plum she'd taken from the fruit bowl. The juice dripped over her chin and she wiped it away, making her fingers sticky. When she'd trimmed down to the stone, she popped it in her mouth, sucking until every last tendril was gone, her tongue shifting against the surface. The sensation was familiar, like sucking her thumb. She rejected the thought and spat out the stone but it landed on her foot and she kicked it away.

From the bench, Deana sat and watched the comings and goings on the bus. She knew most of their names: Søren, the white-haired Dane, and Ray, the Aussie with a fluffy moustache. There were a handful of Judiths, each given a new identity by nickname, and Katy, the primary teacher who launched into song. Squinting to get a better view, Deana studied the downstairs windows, where silhouettes lurched as music from the CD player seeped. She waited for the air-guitar action to start and smirked at the now familiar performance. But smiling made her remember there was nothing to be happy about. Brett could be one of the guys larking about and there was no way she'd find him amusing. Her thoughts circled. *Maybe I've got the clap, maybe I deserved it.*

Katy appeared on the platform of the bus, weighed down by a large colander and a supermarket bag. She made for a patch of sun and sat on the grass shelling peas. A couple of girls chatted on their way to the shower block, their towels trailing the ground. *I'd like Katy to be my friend. If I offer to help with dinner, that'll be a start. And I'm on the rota for washing up with Ray tonight, that'll build some bridges.* Collecting the unread book that she carried around like a security blanket, Deana walked back.

'Can I give you a hand, Katy?'

'I'm nearly done here. But you can help with the spuds.'

'Okay, where are they?' Deana tugged at the plastic bag.

'I've washed them already, they're in the sink.'

'Oh,' Deana hesitated. 'That'd be inside?'

'Of course. What's wrong?'

'Well, nothing. It's just that all the boys are in the bus.'

'Don't let them put you off,' said Katy. 'I'll come in with you.'

Camouflaged by the fug in the lower deck, Deana sorted the potatoes: large ones for baking, small for mashing. She saw Brett take the last drag on a joint and he stubbed the end in an ashtray. He showed the silver glint of fillings as he yawned. Deana rattled the cutlery drawer as she searched for a knife and Katy worked the peeler. Concentrating on chopping, Deana missed the joke but joined the laughter, her breath exhaling like rapid fire from a machine gun. Then a shout went up, the boys tumbled out of the booths and jogged through the bus as if moving from the start line. Deana flattened against the kitchen units, allowing them to push through, feet in slapping flip flops making for the exit. *Maybe I should call then thongs, use the language of the Aussies and I'll feel more like one of the group.*

Brett was the last to leave. He sauntered along the aisle. She noted his familiar underarm smell as his freckled fingers squeezed her wrist. Katy continued to hum as she worked.

'G'day.' Brett released his hold and left the bus.

'See you later,' Katy called after him.

Deana hung her head, studying the dusty fingerprints that marked her skin like a handcuff.

Belemnite

The wind lashes my cheeks and strands of untamed hair escape from my scarf. False footed by the incline, I lose my nerve and shelter by the rocks. But Archie strides the beach, his eyes fixed to the ground. Each time he shows a specimen to the expert, his shoulders hunch when the bearded man shakes his head. Other fossil hunters in flapping raincoats scurry like crabs, picking and turning pebbles. Screwed up with anticipation, Archie continues to look, forcing over boulders too heavy to carry, examining the stones like jewels beneath. When it's time to walk back, he stiffens, shoving his hands in his pockets, shrugging off the arm I place around his shoulders. With his elbows sticking out like wings, he bends over and concentrates on searching with each step. The others wander off, but I stay and watch him, my face wet with drizzle. At a rock pool he drops to his knees, the water like obscured glass, he trails a finger through the weeds and shells. Removing a cylinder of black stone, he runs along the shingle to catch up with the guide.

As he walks back he smiles, his wet hair is springy with curls and there's a glint in his navy rimmed eyes.

'It's a Belemnite, Mum.' Archie places the bullet-shaped fossil in my hand; I turn it over, studying the surface marked with indents.

'Well done, Archie. Now you can start a collection.'

'Naah.' He crinkles his nose. 'It's a present for you.'

Roger's Seat

He studied the sand-coloured blocks of the church that formed the wall and vowed that he'd never go inside. Scanning the street he looked for a pub, refuge for the hour's wait. There was a café opposite but that was no substitute, even if he could muster the energy to make it across the road. He sank onto the brick wall. The others could do their duty if they wanted – his principles would never allow it. Combing his beard with his fingers, he counted the cars as they passed and drank the exhaust fumes. The metal strap of his watch spun around his wrist where it once fitted snugly, but that was ten maybe fifteen years ago. The afternoon sun made him squint and he sat there in a swelter, the heat stoking his anger.

He wore a tie to look smart for his sister but even the task of loosening it was beyond him. His fingers didn't work the way they used to and he folded his arms, keeping his hands out of sight. Coughing, he spat phlegm into the gutter and he looked around to check whether anyone was watching. He'd give them a bollocking if they dared cross him. Today was not the time for showing a weakness.

Marjorie was one of the first out. He might've guessed she'd make a hasty retreat. Not her sort of thing either, but she was more pliable than he'd ever been. Her face had weathered with all the worry, although she managed to pull a smile when she saw him.

'You are coming to the crematorium, aren't you?' she asked. 'You've made your point about not going in the church.'

'I knew her all my life. I knew her the longest out of all of them. Probably means I knew her the best. But did they ask my opinion? No.'

'She was my sister *too*.' Marjorie offered her hand and he clamped his palm to it, dragging her sideways as he got to his feet.

'I'll ride in the hearse with my sister in the box. It's what she would've wanted.'

'I'm not sure there's a spare seat, Roger. The girls have it all planned but I can ask, if you like.'

'It's my rightful place – my entitlement.' He waved his fist in the air.

'Stop making a show of yourself.' It was his daughter who spoke from under the rim of her hat. 'Trust you to make a difficult situation even worse.'

'She was my sister,' he raged. 'I'll take no fucking lip from you.'

'Listen, Dad, you get in my car, it's just around the corner. We can follow the hearse.'

'Don't you start on me. You're as bad as the rest of them. You're nothing but a turn-coat.'

'What d'you mean by that?'

'Bloody Catholics – I hate every one of them.'

'Any more than Jews? Any less than Blacks?'

'Don't get him going again,' said Marjorie.

Friends

Most of the boxes are unpacked and when I've finished cleaning my bedroom, I'll put up the last of the curtains. The hems will hover above the sills but they'll remind me of our old house, of our old life. I screw the newspaper into a ball and swipe it over the just-washed window, removing the streaks and smears. When my arm begins to ache, I lean on the frame and stare outside. My son's walking home: his shirt's tucked in but for a flap at the side. The tie is his only form of self expression and he wears it showing a tiny knot and a long tail. With his mates, he barges along the path, his bag swinging. He shouts goodbye as he turns towards our front door and I hear the key in the lock.

Peeling off the rubber gloves, I call downstairs and follow my voice as it bounces off the walls. Entering the kitchen, I see Dan taking gulps from the milk bottle.

'Use a glass,' I say.

'There's no need, I'm going to finish it.' He grinds the empty bottle on the table.

'Good day at school?'

'Yeah, I suppose.'

'You looked happy walking home. Who were those boys?'

'Mike and Jay – they live round the corner.'

'Oh.' I think of the times I've nodded and smiled at the neighbours but they don't make newcomers feel welcome around here. 'You've got your Dad's knack for being friendly. He'd have been proud of you.'

'I know.' Dan smiles and moves towards me, his arms outstretched. 'Have a hug. You'll soon get to meet people too.'

'I'm not so sure.' While I'm smothered in his arms, a tear falls. I wipe it away as he releases me and hide my face with my fringe. 'Have you got any tips for making friends?'

'Nobody's ever asked me that before.'

I stare at the wall and talk to the cobwebs. 'I need to know because I'm desperate.'

'Don't worry, Mum, it'll be okay. Just try talking, talk to anyone.'

'I'm not used to doing that.'

'Or you could try walking into someone – make it look like an accident – and start a conversation from there.'

'Good idea.' I disguise a giggle by starting to cough. 'I better get on with sorting my room.'

'You can do it, Mum.' Dan calls after me. 'I know you can.'

Through the sparkly glass, I watch the walkers on the street. A grey-haired woman swings a plastic bag with dog poo inside while the puppy pulls the lead and sniffs the grass verge. There's a man dragging a shopping trolley behind him. Holding her toddler's hand, a mother finds a gap in the traffic to cross the road. I imagine using Dan's accidentally bumping into someone strategy, and laugh. The curtains need hanging and I get on with the chores.

Walk Over Me

In a cocoon of warmth and quiet, I slide my fingers under the airing cupboard door and pull it flush with the frame so that only a slither of light enters the midnight space. I retreat from my husband, from the life that we've made. I sit cross-legged and wait. Wait to be consumed by the still small thoughts of the child within.

I had a secret place under the stairs that led to my big sister's room. I crawled along a strip of moulting carpet to find the biscuit tin hidden under the first step. I sorted my treasures by torchlight: some favourite cards from birthdays past, a collection of milk teeth, pieces of glass turned to jewels on the beach, a plait of silky ribbons. Once I'd organised the pieces, I put the tin aside and lay flat on my back. With my spine straight against the floor, I'd wriggle my head into the space where the tin fitted. The tip of my nose scraped the wood, my breath was warm and damp. I pulled my knees up, jamming my legs under the fourth step. And there in the dark, I did my listening.

Whoever trod the stairs didn't realise they were walking right over me. My sister shifted the balls of her feet as she walked, as if stubbing out a cigarette right on my face. Taking the steps two at a time, my brother's feet caught the edge of the carpet runner, first on the left side then the right. He didn't step on me at all. When he came to the wedge that turned the corner to her room, it winced under his weight and I sensed his feet slipping in his socks. He hovered at the doorway, deciding whether to knock. Usually she guessed he was there and swung the door open. Traces of their voices came to me, thin laugher, or the stumble and bump of teenage wrestling.

M never went up the stairs, she stood on the landing and called. She said to my sister, 'Come down now. I want to talk to you.' Then she shouted in a high-pitched voice, 'I'm not going to call you again.' I sniggered while the silence lasted. 'If you don't come down now, you'll have no dinner.' My sister had learnt to do as she was told and I was smug in my secret space. It was different with D. He slapped me in the face every time he went up. He took the stairs steadily, getting ready for a row.

Punching the door open, he bellowed at my sister, and cursed. She was one of the three reasons his life didn't measure up to much. I quivered and held my breath while he turned around. On the way back down, I heard his shoes straining, the leather groaning, someone was in for it.

I coax the child from her hiding place, my voice murmuring and soft. Wrapping my arms around her frame, I ease her next to me. Tracing the notches of her spine, I walk my fingers along the bones, counting them right down to her waist. Her head rests on my shoulder and we breathe in time. I stroke the fine strands of her hair, arranging the ringlets behind my ear. I wait until the moment is ripe. Respect your inner child, my adult voice says.

Russian Wedding Ring

Twisting the ring around her little finger, the interlocking bands of white, gold and rose rubbed against each other. Sheila rolled them over her knuckle then spread them out, as if trying to work out how to make them separate. When her moment of musing was done, she pushed the rings back into place and finished her cup of coffee.

It was raining and the windows of the café were beginning to fog. People scuttled the street like beetles, crouched under umbrellas and hunched against the wind. The lunchtime queue at the counter was thinning and a couple of the tables were littered with the debris of dirty crockery and smears of ketchup. Thea was always late, juggling appointments and taking important calls now she'd joined the management team at the shop. It was clear Sheila had dropped down her daughter's list of priorities. Noting the twang of rejection, Sheila folded her arms. It was only right. Thea had always been good with numbers. She'd make her own way in the world.

When the door opened, Thea poked her head through the gap and smiled. Her hair was a mass of ringlets, an investment at the hair salon, Sheila guessed. Thea sashayed to the table, propping her umbrella against the wall before pulling out her chair.

'Give us a kiss.' Sheila offered her cheek.

'Okay.' Thea obliged, then took off her jacket and draped it over the back of her chair. 'Oh, I've left a lipstick mark on you.'

'That's typical.' Sheila grabbed the napkin and rubbed her skin. 'You like to leave your mark.'

'Is that meant to be funny?'

'Yes.' Sheila checked her reflection in the window, making sure her face was clean. 'You take offence too easily.'

'Oh.' Thea studied the menu. 'Are you having lunch?'

'No, thanks. Another coffee will do me.'

'I'll see if there's a cake we can share.'

With her skirt flapping as she walked and the bangles on her wrist chiming, Thea went to the counter and placed the order. The cook chatted with her through the kitchen hatch and

Sheila noticed him wink as Thea's giggles carried. Sheila counted the veins on the back of her hand as she waited. The ring caught her attention again, the red gold an exact match to the strawberry blonde of Thea's hair. That was one of the reasons she'd bought it. Den had never given her a ring and then he'd scarpered, so when her number on the premium bonds came up, it was a ring she purchased. A ring to represent her family.

'They'll bring it over in a minute,' said Thea. 'Just enough time to glug the coffee down and get back to the office.'

'That won't do you any good.'

'I'm used to it.' Thea reached for Sheila's hand, cupping it in her own. 'So what did you want to talk to me about, Mum?'

'It's Penny. She's not getting on so well. All I hear from the school is that she's late, she's not done her homework, she's smoking.'

'That's not the end of the world.'

'But it's only a couple of months until her exams. She'll never find a job without any qualifications. She says she's not going to college even though she's been promised a place. She's got a good brain but she doesn't want to use it.'

'Try not to worry.' Thea's phone bleeped in her pocket. She took it out and glanced at the screen, then lined the handset with the edge of the table. 'I'll have a word with her, if you like.'

'I'm not sure you'd even recognise her. She's dyed her hair black.'

'It's just a phase.' This time Thea's telephone trilled. 'I'm sorry, I'm going to have to take this call.' She walked to the door and shivered in the porch, the handset glued to her ear.

The coffee arrived with a large slice of Victoria sponge. Sheila took the top half and began to eat, the sugar sticking to her lips. She knew that the colour of Penny's hair wasn't important, but to sacrifice those blonde locks seemed such a waste. The gold band glinted on Sheila's finger, the band that represented Penny. They'll be no changing it for an ebony ring to match her new hair, that's for sure. Sheila twiddled the rings again, and scoffed at the last one. The white gold was the colour of Sheila's hair, turned swan-like within weeks of Den leaving.

'Sorry about that.' Thea smoothed her skirt and sat.

'I want to talk about your birthday. I want to know what you'd like as a present for your twenty-first.'

'Don't go worrying about that. You've got enough to think about.'

'But I don't want to let the day go by without marking it as a special occasion.'

'Mum, a card will be fine. I really don't need anything. And you've got to be careful with your money. Sick pay doesn't go very far.'

'Don't remind me. I've got an interview with occupational health next month, to see if I'm fit to return to work. Some hopes of that when it's hard enough to get out of bed.'

'You managed it today.'

'That took a major effort.' Sheila rolled the ring over her knuckle and she slid it across the table. 'You'll accept this, won't you? A twenty-first birthday present from your mother. It's symbolic, you know. To remind you of the three of us.'

'I don't need to be reminded.' Thea scooped the ring into her palm and chased it around. She pushed the three rings onto her finger and admired the look of it. 'I'm never going to forget you.'

'I should hope not.' Thea's mobile bleeped, interrupting Sheila. Hesitating, Thea's silver-grey eyes sought permission to read the message. Sheila angled her head and raised her eyebrows. She'd prepared a whole speech to share with Thea.

'It's a text from work, they want me back at the office.' She dropped the mobile into her handbag and took out her lipstick. 'What were you saying, Mum?'

Sheila watched her apply a coat of burgundy to her lips.

'I'll stop my dithering,' said Sheila. 'Have the ring and remember us when you wear it.'

'Thanks.' Thea slung the bag over her shoulder. 'I've got to go. I'll get the bill.'

'There's no need, Thea. I'll pay for this one – you get off.'

Sheila watched her daughter dodge the puddles as she crossed the road. Picking up the bill, she noticed a stripe of pale skin where her ring had been. Her finger was empty now, stripped of decoration, and she withered at the loss. Taking a tissue from her sleeve, she blew her nose. It was time to head for home. Penny would be back from school soon.

Expatriate Wife, Papua New Guinea

The women walk barefoot to market, their heels are cracked and yellow, their long skirts all dusty. They spare me a glance as I run a broom across the veranda, sweeping the clods of dried mud left by my husband's boots. One woman waves, the lines on her palm are a map of the country. A bare-chested man follows, his black skin slicked with pig-fat, his hair and beard merge into one like a balaclava. Wearing a cloth low across his belly, the branches of tangent leaves cover his arse. I wonder, was it you who climbed the perimeter fence in the night and jumped the barbed wire? Was it you who scavenged in the carport and under the back steps? I notice the metal glint of the axe at his waist and I retreat inside. If I knew the words in Tok Pisin, I'd say you're welcome. Have the electrical cable that you wear around your middle as a belt.

Six-word Story

Wanted: gardener to propagate passion seeds.

The Stream

The paper bag is damp in my hand and I peek inside – most of the sherbet pips are stuck together like frogs' spawn. I pull free a chunk and it fizzes on my tongue. Debbie's got rhubarb and custard. She counts the sweets, putting them in a line along her thigh.

'That's not fair.' She talks with a sweet tucked inside her cheek, making her look like a hamster. 'Last time I bought two ounces I got eight sweets, but I've only got six this time.'

'Don't forget the one in your mouth,' I say.

'Oh, yes.' She nods and returns the sweets to the bag, inspecting the yellow and red sides. 'This one's chipped. D'you want it?'

'Let's swap.' I take the sweet from her and spill some loose pips into her palm.

'Is that all I get?' She downs the scattering in one go.

I've been walking home with Debbie for a whole week now. She's nice – she's the friendliest person in my new school. She lives round the corner from me and she says I can call for her in the mornings, if I like. I wish I could sit next to her, but I'm stuck with Sean Ellis. He takes more than his fair share of the desk and he rubs his leg against mine when he gets up from the chair.

'Let's have a look in the stream.' Debbie picks up her satchel and leads the way. I don't have a bag so it's easy for me to scramble over the rocks, but she has to make a path over the dried mud. Once we're by the water, she dares me to walk under the bridge. I look at the sloping sides and water laps right up to the edge.

'I can't. I can't get my sandals wet.'

'You won't get wet. There's enough of a ledge to walk on.' Debbie points. 'I've done it loads of times.'

'You go first then.'

Debbie clutches her satchel and takes side-by-side steps, her back against the concrete wall. I watch her until she says it's time for me to follow. I'm only a couple of paces in when there's a splash. She's dropped her satchel and it's floating down the stream.

'What are you going to do?'

'Get it, of course.' She steps into the ankle deep water, then trots along, chasing the bag. When she catches it, she swings the satchel onto the ground, splattering droplets into the air like a fountain. I find her sitting on the bank, her legs are soaked and she's using a leaf to dry her satchel.

'Aren't you going to check inside?'

Debbie undoes the buckles and finds her pencil-case inside, the new felt-pens are leaking. She takes off her socks and wrings them, then wiping her pens she turns them into a tie-dye of colours.

'Won't your mum mind about your socks?'

'I don't think so,' says Debbie. 'Not if I tell her Sean Ellis pushed me into the stream.'

Packing

1. Clothes
   a. Tops: shirts and hoodies
   b. Jeans: ripped, skinny, bootleg
   c. Skirts: mini, maxi, puff
   d. Bras: underwired and padded
   e. Knickers: pretty ones only
   f. Shoes: heels, flats, Converse
2. Makeup (ditch dried-up nail varnish)
3. Jewellery (silver-dip before packing)
4. Hairdryer and straighteners
5. Pencil case
   a. Highlighters
   b. Gel pens
   c. Retractable pencils
6. Ammonite found at Charmouth (wrap in tissue – put in box with flowers on lid)
7. Paperback (any)
8. Pillowcase with silky trim
9. *Foxy Lady* mug
10. Remember: thermal socks, hot water bottle, Little Ted, ring binder with campus information

Effort

Ready to face the morning, Anna opens the kitchen blinds. Instead of squinting in the sunlight, she puzzles at the puce concoction splattered against the window. Putting on her coat, a Christmas gift from Simon, she ties the belt and goes outside to investigate. There are pink drips marking the wall, fallen from her son's window, and an empty bottle of gin, landed on the lawn.

Only the previous evening, while Patrick played pool in his bedroom, Simon and Anna discussed the future. They decided on a shared New Year's resolution: to support Patrick in achieving his potential.

'We've got to keep him focused for the next six months. Get his GCSEs out of the way. Set him on the path to university,' said Simon.

'Of course.' Anna squirmed, knowing that Simon hadn't fully read Patrick's last school report before she'd squirreled it away. She remembered the comments about Patrick falling asleep in the physics lessons and reading magazines under the table in mathematics. 'So long as he does enough revision, he'll be fine.'

'That's my boy,' said Simon. 'Invest the effort when it's most required.'

With her knuckles poised to hammer on Patrick's door, Anna hesitates. Vomit dribbling down the pebbledash isn't going to score Patrick any points on the road to success. Instead, Anna collects a brush and a bucket and begins the task of cleaning up. Effort when it's most required, she remembers.

You Never Know

Taking a break from pruning roses, I sit on the wall and study the street. The windows of the terraced houses stare over the cars parked bumper to bumper in the residential bays. The bloke that lives two doors along is washing his car, and he nods at me while he sloshes a bucket of clean water over, indicating that the job is done. A bee sounds in my ear then heads for the jasmine bush. I take off my gloves and enjoy the spring sunshine that chases over my arms.

Joel turns the corner into the street, his hair is a mass of dark curls and he's clutching a large, rectangular object. I dread to think what he's bought at the car-boot sale this week. Other kids spend their pocket money on sweets, but Joel's into collecting. He thinks he'll unearth a treasure that no-one else has spotted. I blame my mother: they spend too much time watching antique shows on afternoon TV when Joel's supposed to be doing homework. But I can't complain, she offers the childcare for love not money.

He's got the edge of the painting balanced on his trainer and with each step he moves a little closer to home. I cross the road to help him, and he lets me take one end. It's heavy, the frame is chipped and the canvass spotted with mould. We rest it against the wall and I take a step back to admire his purchase.

'Hmm, is it a ship?' I ask.

'It's a sailing boat out on a wild sea. There are waves blasting against the hull. See the mast leaning? It's likely to be a painting of the Cutty Sark or some other important vessel.'

'How do you know that?'

'Look at the frame.' He points to the place where a label displays the artist's name. 'He's got to be important with a name like War Wick.' I laugh – Joel hasn't learnt how to pronounce Warwick – and he stares at me accusingly.

'That's a giant-sized purchase you've made this week.'

'I know.' He widens his eyes giving a flash of blue and smiles. 'I was lucky to get it.'

'How much did it cost?'

'Two pounds,' he says. 'A man tried to buy if off me once the deal was done. That must mean it's a worth something. He offered me a fiver but I'd said he'd have to go higher than that.'

'Are you sure he wasn't being kind? Didn't want you to be out of pocket with a dud?'

'I don't think so.' His shoulders hunch and I wish I'd never shared my suspicion. 'I thought we could put it in the lounge. It's got a wire to hang it by and everything.'

I'm thrown by Joel's suggestion. There's no way I'm ruining the wallpaper to display that monstrosity.

'Wouldn't it be better in your room? I mean it is your special purchase after all.'

'No.' He stares at the painting. 'I want to share it with you, Mum.'

'You're right, darling.' I swallow my objections. 'Perhaps we can find a place for it in the hall. Important paintings are usually hung above the stairs.'

'D'you really think it's important?'

'It could be.' I choke on my lies. 'You never know.'

'You're right.' He nods his head. 'You never know.'

Six-word Story

Change please. Coins dropped. Smug smile.

Saxophone Player

Performing on the bridge behind Notre Dame, the singer wears a flat cap while his friend plays the saxophone. I linger beside the companion I met while sharing a table for dinner. She's alone in Paris, without any family to consider. Mine are all at home, seething at the way I'm spending my pension on travelling the world. The musicians finish their song and I join the applause. A breeze ripples over my skin and I remove the cardigan draped across my shoulders and put my arms in the sleeves. I wonder whether the singers pay a fee to perform on the bitumen. Displayed on an open suitcase are CDs for sale and the saxophone player asks me over to take a closer look. While I examine the cardboard envelopes, the singer calls to the audience, needing a request for the next song. I select a CD and search in my wallet for a note to pay the saxophone player.

'Do you know, *I've got a crush on you?*' I ask.

'Really?' He blinks. His green eyes should belong to a cat.

'No.' I accept the change he places in my hand. 'I mean the song.'

Sloping Ceiling

Helen lay on the couch beside Rob, resting her head on his shoulder and working her fingers to release the buttons on his shirt. Funny that he never went in for casual wear, he didn't even own a pair of jeans. Halting her progress when she came to the button above his navel, Rob slid her hand away then reached for the remote. Activating the CD player, classical music drifted and Rob whispered nuggets of affection between the tracks. He said Helen was beautiful, that he was lucky to have her and then he said he loved her. Helen's throat tightened, and she wondered how to reply. The boys of her age never had the intensity of someone like Rob.

Milo had been her only real boyfriend and that was back in sixth-form. He'd latched onto Helen because he was the new boy and he ignored the gossip that labelled her as choosy. They walked to school each day and played pool in the common room. On dark February afternoons, they held hands coming home. He took her out for a milkshake one Saturday and she chose the pistachio flavour to demonstrate her sense of adventure.

They kissed a few times before Milo started stroking her breasts. When he plucked at her bra strap, she let him struggle, then she released the hooks with one hand. In his room, they slumped on the bed. The sex was over in three strokes and when Helen stood to straighten her clothes, she became disorientated. Opening her eyes, she found Milo on his knees, praying for her to live. She couldn't understand what was going on until she rubbed her head and found the bruise like a plum where she'd hit the sloping ceiling.

It was probably the accident that kept them together but when Helen grew bored of his gratitude for not actually dying, she ditched him. Milo prayed on that occasion too, hoping to make Helen change her mind, but it didn't work. Once she'd lost her virginity there was little point in holding back and she had sex with whoever wanted it. At least until the time she picked up crabs, but that could've happened when using a public toilet, or so she tried to believe.

After six months of promiscuity Helen found a new focus: success at work. Appointed as an office clerk she became efficient at the filing. She was given a permanent contract and started reporting to Rob. She didn't intend to become involved with anyone, but when he cornered her in the empty office and said he adored her, what else was she to do but open her legs? It would be wrong to deny him, wouldn't it? And now that he loved her, it would be rude to leave a silence hanging. So she filled the gap by uttering the words she'd never said to a man before: I love you too.

City Break

I catch a glimpse of Big Ben as the train draws into Waterloo and the circle of the London Eye is sliced in half by the apartment blocks. With the commuters, I queue by the door and race along the platform. We vie for places through the barriers then flood the concourse. Women in over-sized hats of scarlet and purple are ready for their day at the Ascot horse races. A toddler springs from his buggy and rushes into the arms of waiting grandparents. Herded by their teachers through the crowds, students gabble in French. Notes from the panpipes of a Peruvian band tame the voices. I scan the window displays: dresses and ties, flowers and fruit. Standing under the clock, Judy waits, her hair is in cornrows and her skin's all glossy with cocoa butter. We exchange a kiss and join the others as we barge outside. A pale-faced youth sits crossed-legged on the pavement, whispering for change. I drop coins into his cup and he wishes me a good morning. We walk towards the river where the wind funnels between the buildings. The sun wrestles the clouds, making the concrete glint and bringing us warmth. I suggest we stop for a drink and, sitting at the table, I watch the Thames as the tide churns, making rope-like coils of water.

'D'you miss London?' Judy blows over her coffee then takes a slip.

'Not half,' I reply.

Shedding Skin

Like running a comb through her hair to make a parting, she slices her scalp with the blade. Peeling back three maybe four layers, she finds a silken sheen of hair grown underneath in the darkness. Stripping the skin from her face, she looks in the mirror, waiting for the milky shadows to turn sharp. Her cheeks are pale and her chin bone juts beneath the translucent covering. She tugs the collar of flesh and the seam over her ribs springs open. Her arms escape from the sleeves and she inspects the pads of her fingertips, pink and furrowed as if she's been in a hot bath. She wriggles her hips, pulls up her knees and steps from the skin left crumpled on the floor like dirty clothing. By shedding her skin she's released from shame and the anchors of regret. She's freed from all the things she wished she'd never done. Today her name is Hope.

Seaside

We leave Mummy on the deckchair, her nose already inside the cover of a book, and we race down to the water. Rachel goes into the sea nearly to her knees and Sam jumps the little waves as they roll. Turning back, I head up the beach and grab one of the spades that we dropped on the way. I start to dig but all I've made is a cone of wet sand by the time Rachel and Sam arrive.

'Mia's made a pathetic castle.' Rachel stamps her foot and flattens the pile.

'That's rubbish,' says Sam.

'Can't we make one together?' I ask.

'Okay.' Rachel sends Sam to collect the other spades.

Taking the place in the middle, between my older sister and younger brother, I begin to shovel. As the castle grows, a hole appears, getting deeper and wider. There's a puddle at the bottom and I like its shape, big enough for me to get in. I wonder what it's like to be in the ground with my knees under my chin, my arms wrapped around my legs and the strangeness of sitting in water. I squeeze inside. My skin feels sweaty against the sand and I can just see over the edge. Turning my head, I realise it's the only bit of my body that can move. Everything else is stuck, rammed in place. My lips creep into a smile. This is good. This is mine. I notice Rachel and Sam taking turns at being king of the castle and I don't care that I'm not included.

Soon Rachel gets bored and walks over. 'What're you doing?' she asks.

'Just sitting.' The walls of the hole are beginning to collapse around my shoulders.

'Shall we bury you?'

'If you want.'

They put sand around my neck and quickly my mouth's covered. I'm weighted down, secure in my place.

'Close your eyes,' says Rachel. 'You don't want to get sand in your eyes.'

I do as I am told and enter a world where it's dark and damp. It's getting hard to breath, but I don't mind. I'm good at holding my breath. I am the champion at holding my breath. It's quiet and I'm all alone, but I can still hear Rachel's voice.

'Use the back of your spade like me, Sam. We need to pack the sand around Mia's head so the castle doesn't collapse.'

Daydreams

Fiona paces the kitchen, her heels clinking on the flagstone squares, then she stops and stares through the French windows into the garden. The flowerbeds are bedraggled, the winter frost has killed off any growth and only the potted Christmas tree, discarded on the patio, sprouts a few green needles. Sitting at the kitchen table, Liz snorts at the photographs of fashion mishaps in a magazine.

'What's so funny?' asks Fiona.

'Nothing much.' Liz closes the cover. 'You were never much interested in the lives of celebrities.'

'I'm even more out of the loop now. I was only away for six months but it feels more like six years.'

'You'll catch up soon enough. Once you start university in the autumn, it'll feel like you've never been away.'

'I'm not so sure about that.' Fiona turns back to the window. 'A gap year changes your life, or so the brochures say.'

Watching the sky turn dark, Fiona counts the street lamps as the lemon lights glow. It shouldn't take Ria that long to drive over, but waiting for her is something of a habit that started in the sixth form. Ria likes to make an appearance when everyone has given up hope that she'll make it. Scanning the kitchen, Fiona realises that nothing is familiar anymore, not since Liz's parents completed the renovation. The granite work-surface is cool to touch and reflects the spotlights. Liz has remembered to use a chopping board to prepare the vegetables. The ingredients for the stir-fry appear like an artist's palate: diamonds of orange and yellow peppers, spears of asparagus flown from Peru, circles of courgette with a green frill.

'I'll cook jollof for you one of these days,' says Fiona.

'Will I like it?' asks Liz.

'I ate it all the time in Nigeria. It's a rice dish that's served with chicken. I even got the hang of sucking the bones while I was there.'

'Sounds like you turned native.'

'What's that supposed to mean?'

'Nothing,' says Liz. 'Why don't you keep watch for Ria? I'll make some tea.'

Fiona presses her forehead to the window and as the droplets of rain splatter against the glass, she's transported back to the volunteers' house. Rainfall drops in straight lines in Nigeria and gushes from the corrugated iron roofs. She listens for the sound of the earth licking its lips while she waits for Tobe to arrive, longing to feel his breath on her neck.

I walk barefoot across the wooden planks on the veranda, my cotton dress flaps against my legs as the wind gets up. I'm sheltered from the rain but when the temperature drops, my skin is covered with goose-bumps. I think he'll arrive soon, wrapping me in his arms, threading his fingers through mine, making our skin become like the pattern on a zebra's coat. He has the smell of a man and his soft lips consume me while the tufts of his beard tickle my chin. Arranging the hessian cushions at the unlit end of the veranda, I throw over a blanket ready to hide us from the night. I think of the dark curls on his chest, the loose ones scattering my breasts when our lovemaking is over. I remember how the bedding mat slips as our bodies collide.

'This is hopeless,' says Fiona. 'It's no good waiting for Ria when we've no idea whether she's even going to turn up.'

'She said she was looking forward to seeing you. That she wanted to know all about Nigeria.'

'Forget the tea, Liz. We might as well start on the wine.'

'That's not a bad idea.' Liz takes a bottle from the refrigerator and sets about turning the corkscrew. Placing the bottle between her knees, she pulls her arm in an arc to release the cork. 'I'll pour you a large one, shall I?'

'Yes.' Fiona flicks a switch in her brain, allowing the images to flow. Tobe arrives breathless from dodging the downpour. His shirt is dark with rain, the fabric clings to his ribs, the cuffs are rolled up to his elbows. Diamonds of rain sparkle on his matted hair.

'Take the glass then,' says Liz. 'I can't stand here forever waiting for you to regain consciousness.'

'Sorry. I just phased-out for a minute. You know how it is.' Fiona takes a large gulp that helps to swallow back the lump that's forming in her throat.

'I know how it is with you. One minute you're here, the next minute you're off with the fairies.'

'I can't help it if I like to think.'

'So that's what you call it,' says Liz.

'Anyway, at least I'm here. Which is more than can be said for Ria.'

'She'll be along soon enough. And it's not as if the dinner's going to spoil or anything.'

The night in Nigeria is spoilt. *I search Tobe's ashen face for an answer. I focus on his eyebrows, his eyes would be the undoing of me. Those brown eyes that hold my love, the whites like a rich cream. He rubs his chin and the bristles scrape. I know what he is going to say but I can't believe it's over.*

Fiona walks to the window and, noticing her reflection in the glass, she swings her hips as if modelling on a catwalk. Her figure hasn't changed much in spite of the circumstances. Tracing a finger over her belly, she wonders how long it will be before the pregnancy shows. She imagines her babe, content in amniotic fluid, taking the looks of his father: brown eyes and long straight lashes.

'The rain's lashing down and I can't see a thing,' says Fiona.

'There are headlights on the road.' Liz points towards the street. 'You're not much of a look-out if you can't even see there's a car.'

'If it's Ria she'll get soaked,' says Fiona.

'Of course it's Ria. I'll dash out with an umbrella. You wait here and guard the wine.'

I am on guard, I guard myself from Tobe. I keep the child secret — safe from rejection. And I keep my dreams alive. One day Tobe will come and find me. Find us.

Stone

The dining room is laid with paper cloths and napkins. In my pocket, the stone slips between my fingers, the surface smooth and cool. I found it in the garden as I shuffled along the path. I think of Laura and her tender gaze, her eyes watching my mouth as she tries to understand the words that I dribble. I place the distorted heart on the table where she sits, a stone love letter.

Four Buses in the Desert

November 1981

When Liam suggested we slept top to toe in one of the booths that converted into a double bed, I never imagined all five of us would squeeze into the space. There was little room to move but at least we were warm with the sleeping bags piled on top. In the morning, plumes of breath issued as we spoke and Lynn used the water in the kettle to make a brew. My fingers tingled as I wrapped them around the enamel cup and my throat became hot from the liquid.

Peter banged on the door to gain entrance then barged through the bus. He brushed snow off his shoulders and tapped a tune with his clogs, the only form of covered shoe he possessed. Through his whiskers his teeth chattered but he managed to explain that one of the buses was already in Iran and waiting for us on the other side.

'We'll travel in convoy.' Peter was an employee of the tour company and advised us on safety. 'That way we'll only need one revolutionary guard to accompany us and when we're on the road, we'll make straight for Pakistan.'

'Ready when you are.' Liam tapped his forehead in a salute. 'The driving'll be easier when we get out of these freezing conditions. I can't wait to see the back of Turkey.' He spoke as if he knew what he was doing when really he was a novice who'd volunteered to drive the double decker when the other group of travellers had abandoned it on the border, for want of transit visas.

'There's only desert ahead of us, and a few hostile Iranians to contend with. You and Greg are doing a great job with driving the extra buses. Pity we can't put you on the payroll for your efforts.'

'No worries,' said Liam. 'You can buy me a buffalo steak dinner when we reach Nepal.'

When the trucks at the front of the line started their engines, we weren't far behind, and at passport control Liam left the engine running while we filed through the office. The truck drivers elbowed their way past and we followed. At least they knew the routine and we copied, opening our passports to the page with the stamped visa and nodding our heads. My scarf fell into my face with every gesture, my hair was too fine to keep the fabric in place, but I learnt to restrict my movements as the days passed. My fair complexion made me a target for accusations of being American even when I used my best BBC accent.

No-one dared challenge the revolutionary guard, even when he directed the convoy to drive through the centre of Tehran. It wasn't part of the plan to go through the capital, a few blocks from where the American hostages had been held and their release only secured at the beginning of the year. We drove alongside the splayed legs of the white tower that was the symbol of Tehran, constructed to celebrate the Shahs and marked with graffiti in Farsi and sprayed with images of the Ayatollah. In the city, the women wore Western clothes and waved at us as we stared through the bus windows. In the rural areas, the women's oval faces were cloaked by the hijab and groups barged the stationary bus when we needed to buy fuel. Men and children taunted and waved their clenched fists, believing us to be an enemy. We edged away from the windows and ducked. With their palms planted on the glass, they rocked the bus, meaning to topple us, but all they left were handprints as the engine gurgled then rattled and we moved off.

Only on unused roads did we stop again. Peter decided when we should eat or camp and gave the orders. We'd grab some exercise by walking around the bus a few times, then we'd take to our bunks for a kip. The boys took shifts at driving and once when the road ran beside a stream we stopped. It was safe for the men to take a dip but we girls only washed our hands and faces.

We saw a tower in the desert on the fourth day of driving and we knew the bulk of the country was behind us. The Naderi Tower in Fahraj was built from interlaced bricks, to guide camel caravans in the region of Bam. To do this a fire was lit on top of the high stump and charcoal ashes littered the ground all around. Most of our party climbed the tower, to see the view of the desert, but for Peter it was more important to check that the roofs of the buses had sustained no damage while going under low bridges.

'I dunno.' Liam shielded his eyes from the sun with his hand. 'You wait for a bus in the desert, then four come along.'

Six-word Story

'Tickets please.'

Frantic search.

Fine paid.

Cutting Loose

Gary lives on Wahroonga Drive although not in one of the Queenslander houses, where the veranda loops the weatherboard walls like the brim on a hat. His home is a rabbit hutch at the other end, squat against the ground, with a tin roof turned to the colour of chalk. He invited me half way round the world for Christmas and now it turns out that I'm here to help with the renovations. With my Dad being a carpenter – he guessed I'd know a bit about the trade – Gary's a mate but he's got a nerve. There's running water but the tap's outside the back door and there's a handy tree to piss behind, which is better than facing the bathroom. The avocado suite is enough to turn your stomach and that's without looking at the pan too closely.

I've got up early to make a brew and I plug the kettle into the single socket hanging by the wires from a hole the size of my fist. Once I've made the drinks, I carry the mugs to the bedroom. The black tea slops as I walk along the passage, adding another stain to the bare wood floor. I'm getting used to drinking tea without milk. Gary hasn't got a refrigerator but he's proud of his Eski packed with ice. Only it's filled with cans for the holiday; beer takes priority over a decent cuppa in Gary's world.

'Wake up, Gary. It's Christmas Day.' Pushing the bedroom door open with my foot, I squeeze through the gap and my T-shirt catches on a nail. I'm stuck to the wall and I try to get free but the tea scalds my hands as the liquid spills. Gary's mattress is on the floor and within kicking distance. With my trainer, I nudge his calf. 'Wake up, sleepy head.' He lets out a snort and turns over. There's nothing for it, I give him a kick right where a blue vein snakes around his knee and he yelps. 'Help me. I'm stuck.'

'Don't be such a wuss, Neil.' He talks but doesn't open his eyes. The ceiling fan's the only thing that moves, slicing through the fug of stale breath and body odour.

'D'you want your tea or don't ya?' That gets him to his knees and he pulls up his boxers to cover his fat arse. Stumbling forward, he reaches for a mug and takes a slurp.

Then he sits on the mattress, his legs crossed like he's going to practise yoga. I unhook my T-shirt and examine the snag in the middle of my chest. 'Call me Scaramanga, why don't you?' I point to the hole.

'What?' Gary digs sleep from his eyes. 'It's too early in the morning for me, mate.'

'You've seen *The Man with the Gold Gun*? You must've. I thought you were a James Bond fan.'

'Course I am.' He squints and I can almost hear the cogs in his mind whirring. 'I get it now – third nipple.'

Over the assault course of pillows and towels, lengths of wood and bits of metal, I make it to the window. The view's not up to much: the yard's a dumping ground for broken tiles and bent nails. Rain splatters on the drive, turning the paving silver. Around the property the fence gives a gap-tooth smile like a Halloween lantern. I look straight ahead towards the bay and a pelican glides with dangling legs, landing on a lamp post. It turns its beak from side to side, making its great saggy throat waggle. I think about my Dad's double chin and how it bulges when he swallows. This is the first year I'm not going to eat a turkey dinner with my father. He keeps up the rituals, following my mother's recipe for plum pudding, and burning the roast spuds, just as she did. I couldn't face the silence in the kitchen, the chair askance as if she's going to walk in any minute. But her place isn't laid, there's no paper napkin, no cutlery spread out. She's not coming back.

He said he'd be all right on his own. That he'd get a chicken rather than a turkey and he'd buy half the items on the shopping list. He said that I should make the most of my chances. That not everyone has kept in touch with gap-year friends and that going to the other side of the world was his ambition, once. But it's a grey summer's day in Brisbane and it doesn't feel like Christmas.

'Is it still raining?' asks Gary.

'Chucking it down.'

'Never mind, mate. It's like home from home for you, isn't it?'

'I don't know what the weather's doing in London. But at least it's warm here, even if it's not dry.' I slap the side of my face to swat a mosquito. 'Gotcha.' I inspect the smear of blood on my palm.

'That's the spirit, mate. Glass half full.'

'So, what are we doing today?'

'You're in luck. I found the electric fry-pan in the shed. I'm going to give you the works for breakfast. You like fried eggs, don't you? And I've got some fresh English muffins stashed way. After that, we'll shoot off to my folks for lunch. They're preparing an Aussie Christmas buffet in your honour. There'll be tiger prawns and crab sticks, cold meats and loads of salads. You'll be stuffed by the end of the day.'

'Things really are looking up.'

'It'll be a Christmas to remember. You're up for joining a table tennis competition, aren't you? It's a family tradition, only make sure my brother's kids get a chance to win. There'll be murder if they don't get to tap the ball.'

'No worries, mate.' I realise I'm beginning to sound like Gary.

When he comes back from his shower, he shakes his head as if he's a dog trying to get dry and sprays the walls with water. I hear him rummaging in the cupboards and realise he's making a start on breakfast. Seizing the chance, I grab his laptop from under the chair. I brush dust from the keyboard and press the start button, then a screensaver appears showing Gary in cricket whites.

'It's all right with you if I send a couple of emails?'

'You go for it,' he says. 'What do you think of me in my cricket gear?'

'You look the part. I never knew you played. You're full of surprises.'

'Too right, mate.' I've received an email from Dad. I was amazed when he got himself a computer and managed to learn the basics through a 'silver surfer' course at the library. Dad sends me his very best Christmas greetings and says he's going round to Jack's house for lunch. This is unheard of. Dad's never wanted to spend Christmas away from his own hearth, at least that's what he's been saying for years. As soon as my back's turned, he's round at his mate's place, and he'll be knocking back the ginger wine at a fair pace, I'll bet.

Gary carries my breakfast over, his towel is now draped across his shoulder like he's a waiter in a restaurant. I push the laptop aside and take the plate. It's not a paper one today but a real, breakable piece of china. The rim's chipped and the pattern of bows around the edge is fading, but I overlook the shortcomings. He offers me a knife and fork and a piece of kitchen roll to put on my lap. There's no eating with my fingers today.

'I've turned your eggs over-easy, the way you like them. I remember your breakfast order from that café in Koh Samui. It's proper tucker for Christmas Day.' The eggs are served on rounds of muffin and he's cut up a tomato and arranged the slices in a pile. On top there's a sprig of parsley, the finishing touch.

'How did you manage all this?'

Gary doesn't answer. He taps the side of his nose with his finger and he watches while I load my fork.

'This is great. Are you going to have some?'

'After you've finished I'll dish up mine. We have to take it in turns with the plate.' Gary looks around the room. 'It's not so bad, is it mate? I mean, the house is getting there.' He looks at the laptop. 'What's the news from home?'

'My Dad's going to his friend's house for Christmas dinner.'

'Is he okay?' asks Gary. 'D'you wish you were back there?'

'He'll be fine,' I say between mouthfuls. 'And there's no way I'd want to miss out on Gary's special Christmas brekkie.'

The big bloke smiles, chuffed at the compliment.

Windmills

Tucked in the pram, the baby finds his thumb, and after a few minutes his eyes close and his fist hangs in the air, as if he's hitching a ride. A weak sun pierces the clouds then vanishes. The sea is slate-grey and flat but at the shoreline the waves churn, offering percussion to the seagulls that squawk and wheel overhead. I walk along the path and my stomach hangs like a shopping bag, disfigured. With each step the stitches pull. Finding a bench, I catch my breath and the baby stirs. I grip the handlebar and jiggle the pram's frame, but he's awake and already screaming. I count the waves as they turn, and when I look back his face is red and mottled like a skinned rabbit and his eyes bulge. I stagger to my feet and start walking again.

A blue-rinse pensioner watches me through the café window. She smiles and acknowledges me as a new mother. Turning the pram around, I drift away. By the kiosk, the children's windmills spin. I remember the ones I stuck into sandcastles when my Dad was the best builder on the beach. The plastic heads hum as they twirl, reminding me of being zipped into my sleeping bag and Dad's bristly goodnight kisses. I hand over the coins and choose a yellow windmill with black stripes. The baby watches as the blades turn, flapping his arms while his 'O'-shaped lips blow bubbles.

'Like the windmill, do you, Nicholas?'

Puppeteer's man

I drop my hands and set the puppet loose. He races for freedom, the strings trailing like reigns, the rings clattering across the hearth stones. Squeezing under the door, the little man escapes. My fingers remain poised, as if I'm holding a cup of tea. I inspect the skin on the back of my hands, noticing the spread of brown spots and the veins erupting. The cloak is heavy on my shoulders and I trace the line of embroidery that secures the edge of cloth. The knot of thread comes free when pick it, and I set about finding a needle and thread, meaning to stop the stitches unravelling.

My hand wavers as I hold the needle to the light. I've wrapped the thread around my thumb, making the flesh bulge between the coils, and the pulse of blood steadies me. I glance in the mirror, my hair's like snow and it trails away from my forehead. A few stands dangle over my right eye, the one that rotates in the socket, spinning on an invisible axis. Balancing the heel of my palm against my chin and I aim the needle. The eyeball needs something to skewer it in place.

Bloody tears streak my cheek and I wipe them away with my handkerchief, making a smeary pattern appear on the cloth. I lean on the mantelpiece, my elbows taking the weight. There are footsteps on the gravel path outside, stones scattering. I turn my blind eye to the window and listen. A scratchy voice says: run, run as fast as you can, you can't catch me, I'm the puppeteer's man.